Dumpling Days

A novel by
Grace Lin

LB

LITTLE, BROWN AND COMPANY
New York Boston

W9-ATJ-223

This book is a work of fiction. Names, characters, places, and incidents are the product of the author's imagination or are used fictitiously. Any resemblance to actual events, locales, or persons, living or dead, is coincidental.

Copyright © 2012 by Grace Lin
Behind the Story © 2019 by Grace Lin

Cover photo © SensorSpot/Getty Images. Cover design by Liz Casal.
Cover © 2019 Hachette Book Group, Inc.

Hachette Book Group supports the right to free expression and the value of copyright. The purpose of copyright is to encourage writers and artists to produce the creative works that enrich our culture.

The scanning, uploading, and distribution of this book without permission is a theft of the author's intellectual property. If you would like permission to use material from the book (other than for review purposes), please contact permissions@hbgusa.com. Thank you for your support of the author's rights.

Little, Brown and Company
Hachette Book Group
1290 Avenue of the Americas, New York, NY 10104
Visit us at LBYR.com

Originally published in hardcover and ebook by Little, Brown and Company in January 2012
Paperback Reissue Edition: March 2019

Little, Brown and Company is a division of Hachette Book Group, Inc.
The Little, Brown name and logo are trademarks of Hachette Book Group, Inc.

The publisher is not responsible for websites (or their content)
that are not owned by the publisher.

The Library of Congress has cataloged the hardcover edition as follows:
Lin, Grace.
Dumpling days / by Grace Lin.—1st ed.
p. cm.
Summary: When Pacy, her two sisters, and their parents go to Taiwan to celebrate Grandma's sixtieth birthday, the girls learn a great deal about their heritage.
ISBN-13: 978-0-316-12590-1 (hc) / 978-0-316-12589-5 (pb)
[1. Taiwan—Fiction. 2. Family life—Taiwan—Fiction. 3. Taiwanese Americans—Fiction.] I. Title.
PZ7.L644Du 2012
[Fic]—dc22

ISBNs: 978-0-316-53133-7 (pbk.), 978-0-316-20385-2 (ebook)

Printed in the United States of America

LSC-H

Printing 5, 2022

To Lissy, who many years ago said
I should write about our first family trip
to Taiwan... and I answered no.

Much gratitude to Mom, Dad, Alvina,
Bethany, Libby, Saho, Neil, and
Christine for making this book possible.

Special thanks to Ann Glass of
Darlington Lower School for her daughter's
inspirational travel stories and to
Felix Chen for his Taiwan memories.

my family on the way to
Taiwan

Chapter 1

A Month in Taiwan

map of Taiwan
(not to scale)

"PINK, PINK, PINK," I SAID OVER KI-KI TO MOM. LISSY, Ki-Ki, and I were sitting next to each other on an airplane, and we were wearing the same hot-pink overall dresses, the color of the neon donut sign in the food court back in the airport. "Why did it have to be pink?"

neon donut sign

"That was the only color they had that was in all three of your sizes," Mom told me. "And I wanted to make sure you matched so it would be easy to keep an eye on you."

"I can keep an eye on myself," I said as I pulled at the brilliant-colored denim. The matching jumpers made it easy for everyone on the airplane to keep an eye on us, and it was embarrassing. Lissy thought so, too.

"I hope no one I know sees me," Lissy had said, horrified.

"I can't believe you're making me wear the same dress as a six-year-old."

"Seven!" Ki-Ki had said. "I'm seven!"

But Mom hadn't listened to even our loudest protests, and now we were on the plane in matching dresses. Whenever people passed us, they smiled and I didn't blame them. We looked ridiculous, like plastic birds in a flock of flying ducks.

"This is an important trip," Dad said. "Traveling is always important—it opens your mind. You take something with you, you leave something behind, and you are forever changed. That is a good trip."

flying airplane

"Yeah, but why does it have to be a trip to Taiwan?" I asked. Dad always spouted in dramatic ways about things, sometimes to be funny but other times because he really meant it. When he meant it, we usually ignored him. "Why couldn't it be a trip to Hawaii? Or California? At least then we could've seen Melody!"

Melody was my best friend, and last year she had moved to California. I wished so much we were going to visit her. But, instead, we were going to Taiwan. Taiwan was far away. It was so far that I wasn't even sure where it was. Mom and Dad called it their homeland. But to me and my sisters, our small town of New Hartford, New York—with its big trees and sprawling

2

lawns, the one shopping mall, and the red brick school with the tall, waving American flag — was our homeland.

our house in New Hartford

I was also grumpy because I had to sit in the exact middle of the row. Mom and Dad sat on either end, Lissy sat next to Dad, and Ki-Ki next to Mom. I was stuck between Lissy and Ki-Ki, and I didn't get to see anything that was going on. "What do you want to see?" Dad said when I complained. "There's nothing to see. You would be just as bored sitting on the end as you would be sitting in the middle."

"And I can't believe we're going to be gone for the whole summer," I said. It seemed so unfair. All my friends at school got to go to fun places for the summer, like the beach or amusement parks. Melody lived near the Universal Studios theme park. *They have a ride there,* she had written me. *It's even better than 3-D. They call it 4-D!*

"It's not the whole summer," Mom said. "It's just one month. Twenty-eight days."

"It's not like you have anything better to do," Lissy said.

"You don't, either!" I said. But she was kind of right. Even though I had other friends, ever since Melody had moved away, my school vacations seemed to drag on like waiting in line at the supermarket. But I still knew I'd rather be at home than go to Taiwan.

"I have lots of things to do," Lissy said with a superior look. "Why can't we leave earlier, like when Dad leaves?"

"I have to leave earlier because I have to work," Dad said before I could say anything to Lissy. "You are the lucky ones! I wish I could stay the whole time."

"Besides, we aren't staying that much longer," Mom said. "Just twelve days more. We want to be there for Grandma's birthday. She's going to be sixty, so it's important."

"Why?" Ki-Ki asked. Ki-Ki was always asking why. Ever since her teacher had told her that there was no such thing as a stupid question, Ki-Ki never stopped asking any. She used to even ask things like "Why is why, why?" Her questions weren't as silly anymore, but she still asked a lot of them.

"Well, remember how there is a Chinese twelve-year cycle — every year is named after a different animal, and it repeats every twelve years?" Mom said. "Grandma is going to be sixty, and that means she has lived through all twelve Chinese animal years five times. That is very lucky."

"Pacy and Ki-Ki, you've never been to Taiwan before. And

Lissy, you were probably too young to remember," Dad said. "We need to go to Taiwan so you will get to know your roots."

"Roots?" Ki-Ki said, swinging her legs to show Dad the bottoms of her feet. "I don't have roots!"

Lissy and I rolled our eyes. Ki-Ki still liked acting like a baby sometimes. Mom said it was because she was the youngest.

"Silly," Mom said. "You know what he means. We want you to see the place where we came from, before we came to the United States."

"You should know Taiwan. It's…" Dad said, his face dimming as he tried to think of the right word in English. His face fell, and he said it in Chinese instead. "It's…Taiwan is…*bao dao*."

Bao dao? I didn't know a lot of Chinese, but that word seemed familiar. It sounded like the Chinese word for…

jiaozi
(dumplings)

"Pork buns!" I said. "Fried dumplings? Taiwan is wrapped meat?"

"No," Mom said, and laughed. "You are thinking of *baozi* and *jiaozi*! I guess *bao dao* does sound a little like the words for pork buns and dumplings. But *bao dao* is completely different. It means 'treasure island.' People call Taiwan an island of treasure."

"Treasure?" Ki-Ki asked. "Is there buried gold there?"

"Well, no, not gold," Dad said. "Treasure like forests and water and rich earth to grow food."

Taiwan suddenly sounded like the woods in our backyard at home. Ki-Ki thought so, too.

5

"Taiwan sounds like camping!" she said. "Is that the treasure?"

I looked at Dad eagerly. Camping was interesting. We had never gone camping. Dad didn't like it. He always said, "What's so good about camping? Who wants to sleep on the ground?" Maybe he would like it if we were camping in Taiwan?

"No! Taiwan is not camping!" Dad said, and we could all tell he was having a hard time thinking of how to explain it. I was disappointed about the camping. "Taiwan is cities and cars and culture and restaurants. In Taiwan, there are beds and good food. A lot of good food!"

"So, food is the treasure of Taiwan?" I asked. I was still thinking about the dumplings.

"Yes!" Dad said, and he and Mom laughed as if I had said something very funny. "Yes, it is! Food probably is one of the treasures of Taiwan. We will definitely eat a lot when we are there."

I heard Lissy give a little sigh. I felt like sighing, too. I'd have to last twenty-eight days in Taiwan until I could come back home. That was so long. Already, it felt like forever.

"Don't worry," Mom said, watching us with a grin. "It will be fun."

"Are you sure?" It wasn't that I thought Mom was lying; it was just that sometimes her kind of fun wasn't the same as mine.

"Yes." Mom smiled. "You'll see."

Chapter 2

On the airplane

airplane window

BEING ON THE AIRPLANE MADE ME FEEL AS IF I WERE stuck in a plastic bottle. It was hard to tell if we had been flying for one hour or ten. At first, we played with the TVs. We all had our own — each was in the back of the seat in front of us, and we could watch any movie we wanted. At home, Mom let us watch only three TV shows a week. We'd each pick one and watch it together, which wasn't always fun. Lissy had just started choosing some silly hospital show with lots of kissing, and Ki-Ki liked a baby cartoon that we (even Ki-Ki herself) were all too old for. So I was excited to be able to watch whatever I wanted.

TV on the back of the airplane seat

But after a while, even that

became dull. I tried to read my books, but my head felt all stuffed up and I couldn't concentrate. Dad was right when he said there was nothing to see. The airplane ride was so long and so boring. It seemed as if the only thing I could do was sleep. Which I did, until Lissy elbowed me awake.

"They're bringing the dinner!" she said. A flight attendant was wheeling a cart and handing out prepacked meals to everyone. I turned the knob that held up my tray table on the seat in front of me. *Clack!* It fell open with a clatter, but no one paid any attention. Everyone was too busy getting the food.

Lissy passed down to me a tray full of covered containers all shiny and smooth. The largest container was wrapped with foil, which I carefully began to peel off. Getting airplane food was fun; it was like opening presents! Though not the most delicious-looking presents. Pale, flattened noodles and unknown meat chunks were drowning in the orange-brown overflow of curry sauce. A mix of sliced cucumbers, corn, and dark purple beans filled one of the small containers. The other container had faded melon cubes, the same color as unripe grapefruit. The dessert was in a wrapper with big white, fancy letters that said CHOCOLATE-CHIP SHORTBREAD, even though it was really just a chocolate-chip cookie.

airplane food

On the side were a napkin; a fork, a knife, and a spoon (all plastic); and a pair of chopsticks. Lissy pushed the chopsticks toward me.

"Since we're going to Taiwan," she said to me, "you'd better learn how to use chopsticks."

"I've eaten with chopsticks lots of times!" I told her. "I know how to use them!"

"No, you don't," Lissy said. "You hold them all wrong."

Did I? No one had ever taught me how to use chopsticks. I had just taken them and eaten with them the best I could. It had worked fine — I had always been able to get food to my mouth.

"Look," Lissy said. "You're supposed to hold them like this. Hold the top one like a pencil. They aren't supposed to cross over like that."

how you are supposed to hold chopsticks

how I hold chopsticks

I tried holding the chopsticks the way Lissy showed me. They felt awkward between my fingers, but I aimed them toward the container of cucumbers and corn and grabbed.

Plop! The slices fell from my chopsticks back into the tray like raindrops. I tried again. *Plop! Plop!* The cucumbers slipped off the chopsticks again.

"See!" Lissy said triumphantly. "You can't use chopsticks! I told you you're going to have to learn!"

"Speaking of learning," Mom said, leaning over, "I found out about a special cultural program they have in Taiwan. It's made just for kids like you — kids from America. We've signed you up for classes."

I stopped trying to pick up cucumbers. Classes sounded like school. Lissy thought so, too, because she made a noise that sounded like she was gargling mouthwash.

"Classes!" Lissy said. "But it's summer. It's vacation!"

"We want to make sure you don't get bored," Dad said.

Lissy, Ki-Ki, and I looked at one another. We all knew never to say we were bored when Dad was around. If we ever complained about having nothing to do, he always said something like "Let me give you some math problems."

"In Taiwan," Mom said, "a lot of kids study in the summer, too. But, anyway, don't worry. We just signed you up for fun classes."

This was another time that I didn't trust Mom's idea of fun.

"What kind of classes?" I asked.

"All different," Mom said. "Lissy has calligraphy, Pacy has painting birds and flowers, and Ki-Ki has paper cutting."

"I can cut paper!" Ki-Ki said. "I don't need a class for that."

"This is special paper cutting," Mom said. "You'll learn how to cut pictures out of paper."

"Isn't calligraphy Chinese words?" Lissy interrupted. "How can I paint Chinese words when I don't even know Chinese?"

"Yeah!" I said. "None of us speak Chinese! How can we take a class in Taiwan?"

"Remember, it's a special program. The teachers will be able to speak English," Mom said. "We were very lucky to find this. Remember that Taiwanese-American convention we went to with Melody's family a couple of years ago? It's run by a group like that. They want to make sure Taiwanese-American kids know about their culture. There is even a special boat tour, but that is for teenagers."

"I'm a teenager! Fourteen is a teenager!" Lissy said. "Why don't I go on that instead?"

"It's for older teenagers," Mom said. "High school."

"I'm almost in high school!" she said. "I could go!"

Lissy was still talking, but I had stopped listening. Lissy was always being boring about how old she was, like we would forget that she was the eldest. But besides that, hearing about the painting class had me worried.

I wasn't worried about actually painting. I was good at art. I wrote and illustrated a book that won four hundred dollars before, and I was going to write and illustrate books when I grew up. I had decided that a couple of years ago. I knew I would be able to paint fine.

But I remembered that Taiwanese-American convention Mom mentioned. Even though I had gone with Melody, I hadn't liked it. It had been horrible. The kids there were Taiwanese-American, and so was I, but they weren't like me at all. In New Hartford, now that Melody had moved, I was the only Asian girl in my class. I tried to be just like everyone else, and I always spoke English, even at home. But at that Taiwanese-American convention, all the girls there could speak Chinese and Taiwanese, and they called me a Twinkie. They said I had lost my culture. "You're yellow on the outside, but white on the inside!" one girl had said to me. "You're a Chinese person who's been Americanized."

And it was true. I was Americanized. In New Hartford, *Americanized* meant being like everyone else and having friends. But at that convention, it meant being humiliated and disliked. Was it going to be like that in Taiwan, too? Would everyone there make fun of me and call me a Twinkie? *Plop!* Another cucumber slipped from my chopsticks onto the tray, and I felt as if it were just like my heart falling.

Chapter 3

Uncle Flower

bouquet
of lilies

I WAS SO SLEEPY WHEN WE FINALLY GOT OFF THE PLANE. We had to wait in a long, long line for something called customs, which was really just a man in a uniform who stamped passports. When we exited, there were crowds of people waiting in front of us. It was like we were walking onto a stage with an audience. But before I could feel scared, we heard a yell and two people ran toward us, waving excitedly, like birds with flapping wings.

"Jin!" Mom said as they ran over to us. Auntie Jin hugged us with a big grin that seemed to stretch across her round face, like a jack-o'-lantern at Halloween. Her husband

Auntie Jin running
toward us

laughed, handed me and Lissy a bouquet of flowers, and took a suitcase from Dad.

Somehow, Auntie Jin herded us out of the airport and into a bus. It was hot! I felt like an ice-cream cone melting as soon as we exited. Luckily, the bus was air-conditioned. Mom and Dad and Auntie Jin and her husband kept talking and laughing in what I guessed was Taiwanese the whole time, though it could've been Chinese — I wasn't sure. Lissy, Ki-Ki, and I sat across from them and looked at the flowers. They were white and pink like stars with raspberry-colored freckles. Their smell seemed to sweeten the air.

"Are they real?" Ki-Ki asked.

"Of course they're real," Lissy said. "Feel the petals. They're lilies."

"Do you think they spray perfume on their flowers here?" I asked. "They smell so strong."

"Maybe," Lissy said, trying to look wise.

"What's our uncle's name?" Ki-Ki asked. "The one who gave us the flowers?"

I shrugged. Lissy looked confused as well. "It's...it's...I know it...."

"You don't know!" I said to her.

"Yes, I do!" Lissy said.

"What is it, then?" I asked.

"It's...it's Uncle Flower," Lissy said.

"No, it's not!" I said.

14

"Yes, it is!" Lissy said, and we all laughed.

"What are you laughing about over there?" Dad asked.

"Nothing," we said as we looked at one another. None of us wanted to ask what Uncle's name was while he was in front of us — then he would know we didn't know it. And that might make us look rude.

"Are you hungry?" Auntie Jin asked us. "Once we get to Grandma's, we can go eat."

"Yes, yes," Uncle Flower said. "First thing you do when you come to Taiwan is eat. Eating is a hobby here in Taiwan."

We grinned at that. Auntie Jin's and Uncle Flower's English was like Mom's and Dad's. It was a little hard to understand what they were saying at first, but once we got used to the way they said the words it wasn't too bad. Besides, they were talking about food, and that was always easy to understand. I was hungry. I had ended up not eating much of the airplane food.

"Okay," I said. "What are we going to eat?"

"Anything," Auntie Jin said. "We're in Taipei, the capital city! It has everything. What do you want to eat?"

"Pizza?" Ki-Ki asked.

"Ki-Ki! Don't pick pizza!" Lissy said. "We're in Taiwan — you have to pick a Chinese food!"

"You don't have to," Uncle Flower said. "There are all kinds of food here in Taipei. We have McDonald's — all that American food, if you want. But Taiwan has the best Japanese and Chinese food — sushi, ramen..."

"Dumplings?" I asked. I remembered how I had mixed up Taiwan being *bao dao* to *jiaozi*, which was a kind of Chinese dumpling. And it was also my favorite Chinese food to eat.

"Dumplings!" Uncle Flower said. "Taiwan has the best dumplings in the world!"

Uncle Flower, Auntie Jin, Mom, and Dad began to speak in Taiwanese to one another really fast. We knew they were all talking about food, and their words sounded like clicking chopsticks. All that talk was making me hungry. I wondered what the best dumplings in the world tasted like.

The bus stopped, and we all got off. So this was Taiwan. I looked at the gray buildings towering overhead and the

Taipei, Taiwan

people and taxis and motor scooters rushing by all around us. So far, all I could tell of Taiwan was that it was very busy. As Dad, Auntie Jin, and Uncle lifted our luggage from the bus, I nudged Mom.

"What's Uncle's name?" I asked her.

"Uncle?" Mom said. "It's Li-Li. He's Uncle Li-Li."

"Lily!" Ki-Ki and I laughed, and Lissy shouted, "I told you he was Uncle Flower!"

Chapter 4

Dumplings in Taiwan

dumpling in spoon

DAD AND UNCLE FLOWER LUGGED OUR SUITCASES UP the stairs behind us while we walked into a roomful of aunties and uncles waiting with hugs. Grandma's and Grandpa's faces wrinkled with smiles as they squeezed each of us at the same time. Although we hadn't seen Grandma and Grandpa in a long time, they still looked the same to me. But we looked different to them. "So tall now!" Grandma said to me, and "Young lady," Grandpa said to Lissy.

There were new cousins, too. One by one, they were introduced to us. Some were just babies, but there were two who were about our age. I couldn't remember everyone's Chinese names right, so I just made up names that sounded close to them. Everyone laughed when I called the sharp-faced boy with the laughing eyes Shogun instead of Xiaoquan and changed his sister's name, Chulian, to Julian. But they didn't really seem to mind, and they still answered when I spoke to them. Shogun was Lissy's age, and Julian was in between my age and Ki-Ki's.

"Speak in English!" Aunt Bea urged them, but they just smiled at us bashfully. "They learn English in school," she told us. "But now they're shy!" She turned to them again. "You can do it!"

Julian looked back and forth like there was a fly in the room. "Hello!" she said finally, and then looked at Shogun for help. He gave a mischievous smile.

"Okay!" he said loudly, and then started to laugh.

"That's it?" Aunt Bea said. Shogun and Julian nodded and laughed harder, and Lissy, Ki-Ki, and I joined in, too. I didn't know if we would be able to talk to the cousins, but I knew I liked them.

"Can you say something in Chinese back?" Auntie Jin asked us. Lissy and Ki-Ki shook their heads hard. We never spoke Chinese in New Hartford, not in school or at home. We didn't know any Chinese words. Well, no, that wasn't true. I did know one Chinese word.

"Jiaozi?" I said.

"Dumplings!" Auntie Jin whooped, and everyone laughed. "I guess that means we should go and eat!"

Everyone laughed again, and the adults began talking about the where and how of dumplings. Finally, something was agreed on, and we followed Grandma, Grandpa, Auntie Jin, and Uncle Flower down the stairs.

Uncle Flower stopped two taxis for us, and we got in.

"Grandma doesn't have a car?" Lissy asked.

"No," Mom said. "You don't need a car in Taipei. It's like New York City. There are so many taxis."

And I realized it did seem a lot like New York City, at least what I could remember of New York City. I had been there only a couple of times with Mom and Dad. But all the bright yellow taxis and the tall buildings and the people walking here were just like it. Except I couldn't read any of the signs. They were all in Chinese.

"Look!" Ki-Ki said to me. "Watch the light!" She was pointing at the crossing light, a flashing sign that told people when it was safe to walk.

But this light had a little green figure walking, like a cartoon. Above him was the countdown of how many seconds left there were to walk across the street. As the number got lower and lower, the figure started walking faster and faster until it was running! When the number got to zero, he turned red and stood still, and our taxi zoomed forward. We laughed. I had never seen a man actually *move* on a walk light before.

When we got to the restaurant, Uncle Flower laughed.

"Usually there is a long, long line," he said. "But we are very early."

"What time is it?" Lissy asked.

"Four o'clock," Mom said. "Are you tired? It is four in the morning at home."

I was tired, but I was also hungry. As we waited for the hostess to seat us, I looked into the kitchen, where the chefs were making dumplings. It was like a fast and frantic dance, the chefs' fingers flying as dumpling after dumpling were made. Six chefs chopped and mixed vegetables and meat. Also in the kitchen were a chef who made the dough, a chef who cut the dough into small pieces, another who rolled out dumpling skins, and a fourth who filled the skins with the meat mixture. And during all of that, more chefs lifted bamboo trays of cooking dumplings out of giant steamers, and hot misty clouds filled the air.

how they make soup dumplings (I don't know where the soup comes from!)

roll the dough

cut the dough

roll chunk into ball

roll ball into flat circle

pick up dough circle

spoon meat filling into center of dough circle

twist closed the dumpling

steam the dumplings and eat!

"They make the dumplings so fast," I said.

"Eh?" Grandma asked. Grandma and Grandpa could speak English okay, but sometimes they had a hard time understanding it. Usually we had to repeat things to them.

"The chefs," I said, speaking slower, "they make the dumplings fast."

"Yes." Grandma nodded. "In China, there is a famous dumpling chef. She can make one million dumplings in seven hours and twenty minutes."

"That's fast!" Lissy said.

"But is it faster than you can eat them?" Dad said. "We'll have to see."

The hostess brought us to a table, and almost as soon as Grandpa was finished ordering, the waiter came out with the dumplings, which were like little pinched bags in a bamboo basket.

Mom put one on a white spoon and handed it to me. I was glad I didn't have to use chopsticks.

"Careful when you eat these," Auntie Jin said. "They're special."

I'd had dumplings lots of times. How special could these be? But as I took a bite, I almost stopped in amazement.

"There's soup in these dumplings!" I said.

All the adults at the table laughed.

"I told you they were special!" Auntie Jin said. "They are called *xiaolongbao*. They have soup inside of them. They're good, aren't they?"

xiaolongbao
(soup dumplings)

I took another bite. The hot soup filled my mouth, and the mixture of soup and meat and dumpling skin seemed to melt into a warm, rich flavor. They *were* good. Very, very good. I began to realize why Uncle Flower said Taiwan had the best dumplings in the world.

They were so good that I didn't even notice that I had soup dribbling down my chin. I quickly wiped it away.

"They say if you can eat these dumplings without making a mess, you are a 'real Chinese' person," Uncle Flower said.

"It's because these dumplings are made so that one side has thinner skin than the other," said Auntie Jin. "And you are supposed to break the dumpling on the thinner side to sip the soup out so you don't make as much of a mess. But they say only a 'real Chinese' person can tell which side has the thinner skin."

A real Chinese person? I bet that meant not a Twinkie like me. But I carefully put another dumpling on my spoon and looked at it closely. To me, the delicate, shiny skin looked the same on all sides. Did this side look a bit paler? Maybe this was the thinner side. I took a bite…and more soup dribbled down my chin. Even the dumpling could tell I was just visiting.

But I could still eat them. I could eat a lot of them and fast. Lissy and Ki-Ki could, too. Grandpa had to place two more orders for us.

"We *can* eat the dumplings as fast as the chefs can make them," I told Dad. "I bet I could eat a million dumplings!"

"If you ate a million dumplings, you would be a dumpling

yourself," Dad said. "You'd be a dumpling stuffed with dumplings!"

Then the waiter came with our dessert. In a round bamboo steamer were nine buns shaped and colored like delicate pink-and-white peaches. They had been so carefully made and decorated that they looked like they had just been picked from a tree. I reached for one.

"These are special peach buns," Auntie Jin told us. "Did you know the peach symbolizes longevity? We are going to have these at Grandma's birthday party, too—to celebrate her long life. You eat these peach buns when you are celebrating something you want to have for a long time."

I took a bite. The peach bun was warm and soft with a creamy, sweet red-bean paste filling. It was good but kind of unexpected. I had thought it was going to taste cool and juicy—like a real peach.

peach buns

"Like all of us being together now, eating these peach buns," Auntie Jin continued, "means that we will be together for a long time."

"And happy," Mom said. "Eating these peach buns while we are happy means we will be happy for a long time."

"Does it mean we'll be eating dumplings for a long time?" I asked. "Does it mean we can have dumplings tomorrow?"

"Tomorrow? And then the next day, too?" Dad teased. "You know, if you have dumplings all the time, you'll get tired of them."

"No, I won't," I insisted. "I could eat dumplings for a long time."

"Well, no matter what," Dad said, "I do know that eating these peach buns after being stuffed with dumplings means we'll be full for a long, long time."

Chapter 5

Visiting Ghosts

fire in barrel

"GET UP!" MOM SAID, SHAKING BOTH KI-KI AND ME.
Ki-Ki made a whining noise and kept sleeping. "It's the
afternoon!"

With my eyes half-closed, I followed Mom and Lissy out of the
room, leaving Ki-Ki alone on the bed. Mom was right. It *was* the
afternoon. We had slept all through the night and the morning,
and now it was already the middle of the day. The bright sun-
light flooded the hallway. I had to rub my eyes as I walked blindly.
When I could see again, I saw the kitchen was full of people.

"Finally awake!" Auntie Jin said, smiling at us.

"Ahh, jet lag," Grandma said, nodding knowingly.

"Jet lag?" I asked. I still felt in a daze.

"It's when your body is all mixed up," Mom said. "When
it's morning here, it's night at home, so your body is confused and you are tired at the wrong time. That's jet lag."

"Oh," I said. My body wasn't the only thing confused. Maybe my brain was jet-lagged, too.

"Anyway, good thing you are finally awake!" Dad said. "We're going out to lunch!"

"We are?" I said. I tried to shake myself to feel more awake. I didn't want to miss any good food. "Can we have dumplings again?"

"You and dumplings," Dad said, laughing. "Well, you can if you want to. We're going for dim sum."

I looked at Lissy. Dad said *dim sum* like we should already know what that was. But I didn't, and, even though she was pretending she did, I could tell by Lissy's face that she didn't, either. Neither one of us wanted to ask in front of everyone and look dumb. I wished Ki-Ki were there. This would have been a perfect time for her to ask questions, like she always did.

But even without Ki-Ki, we would find out soon. Everyone seemed to be in a rush to go, speaking in Taiwanese so quickly that it sounded like a fast-forwarded movie. I was a little surprised when Uncle Flower, Aunt Bea, Grandma, Grandpa, and the cousins got up and left. They must have been really hungry.

"They're going to the restaurant first, to get us a table," Dad told us. "You usually have to wait. This way, we don't waste any time waiting for you to get ready."

"But you still have to hurry," Mom told me. "Go get ready. And wake up Ki-Ki!"

I ran to change out of my pajamas, and by the time I had brushed my teeth and hair, Ki-Ki was almost ready, too. Mom was brushing her hair and helping her put on her shoes at the same time.

As we stepped outside, my tongue fell out of my mouth. It was really hot! The air was thick and sticky, and I felt like a dumpling being cooked in a steamer. I was glad when we got into a taxi. I didn't want to walk, and the taxi was air-conditioned.

taxi

Hundreds of signs in Chinese blurred by during the ride. Red, blue, and green Chinese characters seemed to decorate every surface of the buildings we passed. It was strange not to be able to read anything—it was as if everything were in a code that I felt like I should be able to figure out but couldn't. That kind of made my head hurt. As we drove by another tall building, I saw a metal barrel with black smoke in front of it. Brilliant orange flames burst upward like a flickering flower.

"Fire!" I said, pointing. "Something's on fire!"

Mom, Dad, and Auntie Jin looked and spoke in Taiwanese.

"What?" I asked. "What?"

"It's probably for the Hungry Ghost Festival," Auntie Jin said. "It's almost Ghost Month."

"What's Ghost Month?" Lissy asked.

"Well, it is a little bit like Halloween in the United States,"

Mom said. "It's kind of a Chinese holiday where people honor spirits or ghosts."

"Do you trick-or-treat?" Ki-Ki asked.

"No." Dad laughed. "It's not quite the same. In fact, it's the ghosts who get all the treats during Ghost Month."

"What do you mean?" I asked.

"Well, you know how, in Chinese culture, it's very important to honor one's ancestors?" Dad said. "During the year, families often make offerings to their dead relatives — they make food or burn special 'ghost money' paper for them to have in the spirit world."

"Ghost money?" I said.

"Not just money," Auntie Jin added. "Now people make all sorts of things out of paper — clothes, shoes, computers, even cars. Anything you can think of, they can make it out of special paper for you to burn for the dead. That way, the ghosts can live in luxury, too!"

"So what's Ghost Month, then?" Lissy asked. I was kind of surprised she was interested. She never acted interested in anything, at least not since she became a "teenager."

"Ghost Month is the month that the gates between our world — the living world — and the ghost world are opened," Dad said. "It's the time when all the spirits can come visit their families."

"So what was the burning fire back there for?" I asked.

"When the gates are open, all the spirits can come into the

29

living world," Dad said. "And there are always spirits who have no family to visit—spirits who have been forgotten or lost. We call them hungry ghosts. They wander, poor and starving, because they had no family to feed them or send them money during the rest of the year. So during Ghost Month, people make big plates of food and burn offerings just for them. That burning fire was people giving ghost money to the hungry ghosts."

"Why?" Ki-Ki asked.

"Because people feel sorry for them," Mom said. "And also a little afraid. A starving person is usually a desperate person, so a starving ghost is probably desperate, too. People don't want starving ghosts to make any trouble, so that's why they always make the offerings outside, away from their homes."

"And feed them so well!" Auntie Jin said, laughing. "At some temples, there are hundreds of plates of food, all different kinds."

"Why?" Ki-Ki asked again.

"Maybe because people don't know exactly what food the ghosts like," Dad said. "Spirits can be picky eaters, just like people. Like Great-Uncle Zhuzhan."

HONORING GREAT-UNCLE ZHUZHAN

The Lunar New Year after Great-Uncle Zhuzhan died, we had a grand feast. Our family was doing well: My oldest brother had gotten a promotion at the school he taught at and one of my sisters had gotten married. So for that Lunar New Year, we were able to have a celebration. My mother, sisters, and aunts cooked all day, steaming and frying. I could smell the good food with every breath I took, and I couldn't wait to eat.

In my family, before we ate, we had to honor our ancestors who'd passed away. Since Great-Uncle Zhuzhan had just died, his photo was on the family altar. So in front of his picture, we put the plates of fried dumplings, rice noodles cooked with pork and bean sprouts, a winter melon soup, and even a whole chicken with

family shrine

its head and feet on for extra luck.

Each member of the family lit a stick of incense and bowed three times to the altar, with Great-Uncle Zhuzhan watching us the whole time. Then, when the incense was about one-third burned, Big Brother tossed two coins. We all leaned in to see how they landed. If either coin landed heads up, then that meant our ancestors were laughing and not finished eating yet. It also meant Big Brother would have to keep tossing the coins. Only when both coins landed tails up could we eat.

But on this day, the coins refused to land tails up. Over and over again, the coins landed — sometimes one heads up, sometimes both, but never two tails. The food was getting cold, and I was getting hungrier and hungrier! I felt as if the ancestors were laughing at us!

Everyone else in the family was getting hungry, too. And we were all puzzled. Why weren't the ancestors eating?

Then my aunt made a noise like a firecracker. "It's Zhuzhan!" she said. "He always likes things so salty!"

And she grabbed the rice noodles and rushed back into the kitchen. I watched as she threw the noodles back into her bowl-like frying pan, ladled in more soy sauce, and tossed the mixture over and over again on the stove. Then she dumped it back onto the platter and pushed it toward me to place on the altar. "Now try," she said.

Big Brother threw the coins. Up, up they flew in the air and then — cling, cling — landed on the floor. Our heads bumped into one another as we all crouched to see how they landed. Both tails! Great-Uncle Zhuzhan finally liked the food! And we could finally eat.

"So ghosts have favorite foods and flavors, just like we do," Dad said. "And for the whole month, we try to make them as happy as possible."

"Ghost Month is a whole month," I said, "and we're here for a whole month, too! Are we visiting like the ghosts are?"

"I guess so," Dad said. "Are you hungry?"

Lissy, Ki-Ki, and I looked at one another.

"Yes!" we all said at the same time.

Chapter 6

Eating Dim Sum

egg tarts

I REALLY *WAS* HUNGRY, WHICH WAS WHY I WAS GLAD TO see Uncle Flower, Aunt Bea, Grandma, Grandpa, and the cousins waiting for us at a big round table at the restaurant. It was good they had left earlier, at least good for us, because that meant we could walk past all the people waiting in line and just sit down and eat.

And we began to eat right away! For dim sum, no one ordered from a menu. Food just came to us! Women slowly pushing silver carts went from one table to the next, calling like birds. All the carts had different foods, and as they stopped one by one at our table, Aunt Bea and Uncle Flower would shake their heads or nod. If

food on carts

they shook their heads, the woman would push her cart to the next table. If they nodded, the woman would take a dish out of her cart, put it on the table, and stamp our bill.

"Ha! Dim sum is like a backward buffet," I said. "Instead of going up to the food at a buffet and choosing, the food comes to you!"

"But better than a buffet," Dad said. "See how all the dishes are small? It's so you don't get too full on one dish, so you can taste a little of everything—because there is a lot more to choose from in dim sum than at a buffet."

I looked around the restaurant. There were so many women pushing carts, it was like an endless parade. I tried to count them all, but they kept moving, and there were so many people that I gave up after thirty-eight.

"What do you want to do today?" Aunt Bea asked Mom as she nodded at a woman pushing a cart and held up two fingers. The woman stopped calling out "xia jiao, xia jiao" and placed two small plates on our table. She uncovered them, revealing in each three freshly steamed dumplings with filmy, light skins that showed

xia jiao
(shrimp dumplings)

the delicate pink of the shrimp inside, before wheeling away.

"After brunch, we have to go shopping," Mom said. "We have to buy the art supplies for their art classes tomorrow."

"Tomorrow!" Lissy said. "The classes start already?"

"Yes." Mom nodded.

Shaomai
(pork dumplings)

I was only half paying attention. I was reaching for a brown ball of meat held in a yellow silklike wrapper. *Shaomai*, the cart woman had called it. But it also looked like a dumpling and it looked good. I kept trying to use the chopsticks the "right" way, like how Lissy showed me on the plane, but the food kept slipping.

I looked around the table. No one was paying attention to me. They were all eating or talking or watching for the next cart. I changed the position of my chopsticks so that they were the wrong way, the way I had always held them before. And I grabbed a dumpling. I did it! The wrong way worked, at least for me. The chopsticks gripped the dumpling tightly until I dropped it into my mouth, the rich, savory meat tingling my tongue with flavor. *Yum.*

"What do they need?" Grandma asked. "I have a lot already."

Mom took a list out from her purse. I looked over her shoulder, but since I couldn't read the Chinese writing, I focused my attention on the food. Aunt Bea and Uncle Flower kept nodding at all the carts, and dish after dish were getting placed on the table. Some things I had eaten before—like the snow-white buns bursting with sweet, barbecued pork and the golden-fried rectangles of turnip cake. But there were things I had no idea what they were. I picked up something crispy and brown that looked a bit like a large twig from a tree. Uncle Flower had grabbed it eagerly, and Julian had one on her plate, so I thought I'd try it. It was hard to bite, and even though I was holding my chopsticks better, I ended up grabbing it with my hands and gnawing on it like a puppy with a bone.

"Lissy needs an inkstone and an ink stick. They both need rice paper, brushes…" Mom said, but then she saw me eating. "Pacy, do you like that?"

I stopped in midchew. The twig was kind of chewy and really hard to eat, but the spicy taste was okay. Mom's face looked amused, though, as if I were doing something funny. It made me suspicious. "Why?" I asked.

"It's chicken feet, did you know?" Mom said.

Chicken feet! I was eating chicken feet! *Eww!* I put it back on my plate and made a face.

chicken feet

"*Bawk-bawk!*" Lissy whispered. Mom said something in Taiwanese to the rest of the table, and the adults laughed. But Julian and Shogun gave each other a shrug. Obviously they didn't think eating chicken feet was that weird.

But I felt weird. I kept thinking about chickens scratching in the dirt with their wiry claws, and my mouth felt all rubbery.

Shogun eating at dim sum

I swallowed all the tea in my cup and reached for the teapot for more. Three drops seemed to squeeze out of it, like tears from laughing too hard.

"It's empty," Uncle Flower said, and took the teapot from me. He lifted the lid, turned it upside down, and put the teapot on the table. Almost immediately, a waiter took the teapot and replaced it with another. Uncle Flower tapped his fingers twice on the table.

"Is that a secret code?" I asked.

"What?" Uncle Flower asked.

"Tapping your fingers," I said. "Is that how you got the waiter to give us more tea?"

"No," Uncle Flower said. "Turning the lid upside down told the waiter we needed more tea."

"Then what was the tapping for?" Ki-Ki asked.

teapot with lid on it upside down

"It's a way to say thank-you," Uncle Flower said. "You know that dim sum is not from Taiwan? Like a lot of food and customs here, it is from mainland China. Taiwan has a mix of many cultures — a lot of Chinese, some Japanese, and even a tiny bit of Dutch! Tapping your fingers to say thank-you is from a story in Chinese history."

THANKING THE EMPEROR

A long time ago, the emperor decided to visit his kingdom in disguise. Discarding his brilliant yellow silk robes for the coarse, dull dress of a commoner, he and his advisers (also plainly clothed) stopped at a teahouse for rest and refreshment.

After the waiter placed the small, round teacups on the table, he lifted the teapot high in the air so that the tea flowed like a waterfall. Skillfully, with quick flicks of his wrist, he served the tea without spilling a single drop. The emperor watched with great interest, impressed by the waiter's expertise. After the waiter left, the emperor decided to try pouring the tea himself. As soon as the cups were empty, the emperor grasped the teapot and poured the tea in the same manner for his aides.

Of course, the assistants were incredibly surprised by the act of the great emperor pouring their tea! They were dumb-founded at the honor he had bestowed upon them. They wanted to jump onto their knees and bow low in gratitude, but they knew that such actions would give away the emperor's identity.

Instead, one of the assistants bowed with his

emperor (in disguise)
pouring tea

hands. He curled his two fingers the same way his legs would have bent if he were bowing and tapped the tips of them on the table, in the same manner his head would have knocked on the floor in a kowtow. The other aides quickly copied him, and they all tapped their thanks to the emperor.

"And that became a tradition," Uncle Flower said. "Now, when you want to thank someone for pouring tea, you tap on the table."

All throughout Uncle Flower's story, dishes had continued to arrive on the table and we had continued to eat. As I slowly bit into a sunshine-yellow egg tart, I watched a waiter count up all our dishes to figure out the bill. The flaky crust crumbled, and the bits fluttered down to my plate like falling snow. I put the rest of the tart down. It was delicious, but my tight stomach was telling me

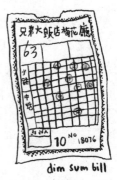

dim sum bill

I had eaten enough. If I had been the emperor's assistant, I would have tapped on the table, too, but only because I was too full to get up.

Chapter 7

The **art Store**

"forever" calligraphy
on wall

AFTER BRUNCH, EVERYONE WENT IN DIFFERENT directions. Uncle Flower and Auntie Jin went to the bookstore; Aunt Bea, Grandpa, Shogun, and Julian went to buy groceries; and Ki-Ki, Lissy, Dad, Mom, Grandma, and I went to the art store. Mom said we were going to take the subway this time because we were getting spoiled taking taxis everywhere.

As we pushed through the crowds to the subway, Ki-Ki hung on to me and I hung on to Lissy. There were so many people! We weren't used to so many people. I felt as if the crowds wanted to crush me away into nothingness.

"Ouch!" Lissy said, shaking me off. "Don't grip me so hard!"

"Sorry!" I said. My fingers were white from clutching her. No wonder it hurt. Lissy looked at me.

"Here," she said, taking a firm grasp of my arm, her annoyance gone. "I'll hold on to you instead, okay?"

Somehow we made it to the subway, Lissy dragging me and me dragging Ki-Ki through the doors. It was only then that I felt like I could finally breathe. After almost running through the hot streets, the cold air of the air-conditioned subway car made me feel as if I were going into a freezer. I was afraid the sweat on my face was going to turn into ice.

Compared with the busy city streets full of cars and black smoke, the subway felt white and shiny. Ki-Ki sat down on one of the molded plastic seats, the color of a bright blue sky, but Lissy and I stayed standing, holding on to one of the gleaming, silver poles. I watched my warped reflection in it as we swayed back and forth with the subway's movement. It was my first time on a subway. Ki-Ki and I had never ridden one before, even when we visited New York City.

me and Lissy on the subway

When we got off the subway, there were fewer people, but it felt even hotter and stickier. When we got to the art store, I felt like a panting dog. The art store was small and crowded, full of papers and shelves. A big fan stood cramped in the corner, its head swinging back and forth quickly like a man shaking his head.

Mom took out the paper from her bag again, and she and Grandma started to speak to the man behind the counter in Taiwanese. As they talked, I wandered around the store. I was looking forward to painting class. I always got an A+ in art in school, and it would be good practice for the pictures I was going to make for books. I decided I'd paint something really beautiful, like a unicorn with big blue flowers. Were there unicorns in Chinese paintings? Probably not. Maybe just a white horse, then.

I walked past piles of paper held down by round, gray-black rocks. The corners of the piles waved at me every time the wind from the fan blew by. Bamboo paintbrushes, the pointed tips looking like cattails, hung from polished wooden racks. Stacks of blue-and-white-painted bowls, dark gray slabs of stone, and ink sticks lay on the shelves with dust.

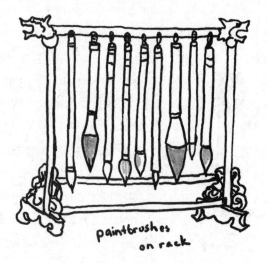

paintbrushes
on rack

At the next aisle, I stopped. Hundreds of little carvings stood in neat rows on the shelf before me. Small stone figures of yawning turtles and snakes, cheerful rabbits, and laughing old men looked back at me from the shelf. I smiled as I looked closer at one figure with a carving of a lazy-looking pig.

Lissy and Ki-Ki followed me.

"Name chops!" Lissy said, taking one and rubbing it with her fingers.

"Name chops?" Ki-Ki asked.

"You know," I said to her, "haven't you seen Mom's in her desk? The ink-stamp thing that has her Chinese name on it?"

"Oh," Ki-Ki said, nodding. "So they're like rubber stamps but made of stone."

"Not exactly," Dad said, coming up from behind us. He had heard us talking. "A name chop is much more important. A name chop is someone's identity. It tells who you are. In the olden days, officials had to carry their seal with them wherever they went."

"Really?" Ki-Ki asked. "Why?"

"The chop was proof that they were the important person they said they were," Dad said. "Everyone has his or her own name chop specially carved only for him or her. It used to be when you signed an important document, you had to stamp it with your name chop as well. They still do that sometimes nowadays."

"What happens if someone steals your chop?" I asked. "Or if you lose it?"

"Ah," Dad said. "Then you are in trouble! You would have a hard time proving that you are who you say you are. Losing your chop would be like losing yourself."

I lifted the chop with the pig on it. The cloudy-gray stone was cold and hard. A shiver ran up my back as I touched the smooth bottom.

"These don't have any names or words," I said, and showed Dad the flat bottom.

"These are probably for people to buy to get their names carved into them," Dad said, picking up a caramel-colored chop with a top shaped like a lotus leaf. "Chinese words and names are an art, you know. It's not like English, where words are made of letters—A-B-C. In Chinese, everything has its own symbol."

"What?" Ki-Ki said. "I don't get it."

Dad pointed at a framed painting of a Chinese word on the wall.

"See that?" he said. "That's *yong*. It means 'forever.' In English, the word *forever* is made up of seven letters, right? In Chinese, that one character is the word *forever*—and that's it. Every object or person has its own symbol."

"So your name chop is your symbol, then?" I asked.

"Yes, in a way," Dad said. "Like I said, your name chop is your identity."

"We don't have chops," Ki-Ki said suddenly. "Does that mean we don't have identities?"

I hadn't thought about that. Did that mean we didn't exist? I didn't like that at all. I wanted an identity! "We need to get chops!" I told Dad, waving the one in my hand. "Can we get them?"

"Yeah," Lissy said, joining in. "It would be a good souvenir."

"Okay, okay," Dad said. "But only one each!"

"Why would we need more than one?" Ki-Ki said. "Unless we decide to become spies and have secret identities!"

"A lot of people have more than one," Dad said, "so they can use whichever chop suits their mood. They sometimes use a poetic phrase or word — anything that they think symbolizes who they are."

"Like what?" I asked.

"I had a teacher who had a chop that said something like 'never too tired for knowledge,'" Dad said. "And my friend had one that said 'thoughts as evergreen as a pine tree.'"

Dad looked at the chops in our hands. "Pacy and Lissy, you should switch. Lissy was born in the Year of the Pig, and Pacy was born in the Year of the Tiger."

We were all a little shocked that Dad was really going to buy the chops for us. Dad never bought us things at home. I gave Lissy the chop with the pig and took the one with the tiger. It was a warm brown, the color of wood. The small tiger's mouth was wide open, showing its teeth. From one side, it looked to me like the tiger was smiling, but from the other, the tiger was scowling. I wasn't sure if I liked it and kind of wanted to pick a different one, but I was afraid that if I did, Dad might change his mind. And I really wanted a chop.

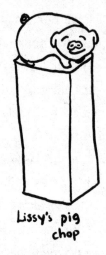

Lissy's pig chop

"And Ki-Ki needs a horse," Dad said, squinting at all the figures on the shelf. "Here's one!"

Ki-Ki grabbed the chop quickly. It was almost pure white, with pale peanut-colored streaks. The carving of her horse

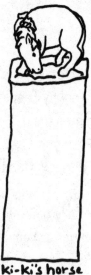

ki-ki's horse chop

looked like the white horses princesses rode in fairy tales, like the one I was planning to paint. I wished I had been born in the Year of the Horse.

We followed Dad as he walked to the counter. Mom and Grandma were still talking to the man there, but now there was a big pile next to them. Lissy, Ki-Ki, and I looked at the rolls of paper and felt, paintbrushes, tubes of paint, and black inkstones and ink stick, and then looked at one another. I wondered which of the stuff was mine.

46

Dad spoke to the man in Taiwanese, and I put my name chop on the counter with the rest of the supplies. I thought Mom and Dad were much more likely to buy it if it was mixed in with the things that they were already buying. Lissy and Ki-Ki did the same.

"We can't get your names carved on them today," Dad said. "They don't do that here. We'll have to take them someplace else. Do you still want to get them?"

"Yes!" we all said together.

"Okay," Dad said. "This way it gives you some time to think about what you want carved on it. Remember, this is your symbol! It is the mark of your identity."

Dad said this in a dramatic way that meant he was joking, but I didn't see what was so funny. Getting my name chop carved seemed really important to me. Even so, I didn't think there was that much to think over.

"I'm just going to get my name," Lissy said. "What else would I do?"

"Yeah," I said. "I'm not going to get anything like 'never too tired for knowledge'!"

"Maybe you should," Dad said. "Then maybe you would get better grades in math."

I made a face. Math was my worst subject, but I didn't do that badly. Just not as good as Lissy and Ki-Ki, who always got A's in math.

"I guess you do need something different. Maybe

something like 'never tired of fun,'" Dad said to me before I could say anything. "Or maybe 'never tired of TV' would be better.... Or ... I've got it! It's the perfect one for you. 'Never tired of dumplings!' How's that?"

Everyone laughed at that. I looked at my name chop on the counter, and it looked like the tiger was laughing, too.

Chapter 8

The Fortune-Teller

my hand

DAD'S NAME CHOP COULD HAVE SAID "NEVER TOO
tired for knowledge," too, because after we left the art store,
he decided to go off on his own to look for a bookstore. I
liked books, too, but since I thought all the books would be in
Chinese, I went with everyone else back to Grandma's.

From the subway to Grandma's house, we had to walk under the street—in kind of a tunnel but one just for people
walking. "These were made because the traffic above is so
crazy," Mom told us. "It's the only way to cross the street
without getting run over!"

There weren't too many people in the tunnel, so I let Mom
and Grandma walk ahead. It was a wide passageway, and on
one side, there were all these women sitting, each with a table in front of her. I stared at them as we walked by. At first I
thought maybe they were offering things for ghosts for the

Ghost Festival, like what Dad had talked about, but most of the tables were bare with just red cloths. Some had note-books and candles, but not much more. There didn't seem to be anything a ghost or a person would be that interested in.

One of the women saw me staring and smiled. For a moment I thought it was Melody's mom, whom I hadn't seen in a long time. She had the same wavy black hair and smile.

The woman beckoned me over, as if she wanted to tell me something. What did she want? It couldn't be Melody's mom—Melody would've told me if her mom was going to be in Taiwan. But still, I had to go over to get a better look. Her moon-shaped face was smooth except for the lines around her mouth, and she had brown freckles on her cheeks, like sprinkles of cinnamon. No, she wasn't Melody's mom. This woman's eyes were different, black and small like watermelon seeds, while Melody's mom had

fortune-teller

eyes that were wide and brown like the color of tree bark. I started to turn away, but the woman grabbed my hand and started to examine it as if she were looking for a splinter.

"Where's Pacy?" I heard Mom say, and I watched Mom and

Grandma turn around. "*Aiya*," Grandma said when she saw me with the woman, which I knew meant she was surprised and not pleased. I started to feel a little nervous then. What was this woman doing? Mom and Grandma both rushed back over to me, Lissy and Ki-Ki tagging behind with excitement.

The woman began to speak to me in Taiwanese. I didn't know what she was saying at all. Mom tried to nudge me away, but the woman's warm, dry fingers held on to my hand tightly. Mom said something to the woman and then Grandma said something, but the woman ignored them. Mom sighed. But since she didn't seem scared, I relaxed. I was starting to feel like I was having an adventure.

The woman traced each one of my fingers, talking the whole time. The short, black curls of her hair didn't move, even when she moved her head to squint at the tips of my fingers. She kept pointing to parts of my hand and saying things to me. She kept nodding and looking at me as if I understood, and somehow it felt rude that I didn't. So I just pretended, nodding and smiling back.

Suddenly, the woman laughed a throaty noise, kind of like a witch's laugh. I thought she might have figured out that I didn't know what she was saying. Without letting go of me, she said something to Mom, who shrugged and nodded. The woman raised her hands over my head, closed her eyes, and started to chant. I glanced over at Lissy and Ki-Ki. They shrugged, and Lissy snorted back a giggle.

She kept chanting an odd song that seemed to roll over me like ocean waves. I stole a look at Mom and Grandma. They didn't look worried or bothered by the woman anymore, just kind of bored.

Finally, the woman stopped chanting and held out her hand. Mom gave her a piece of paper money and pulled at me. The woman nodded good-bye as Mom pushed quickly through the tunnel.

"Pacy, don't do that again! You shouldn't go off with a stranger like that," she said,

Taiwan paper money

shaking her head at me. She wasn't yelling, but I knew she was mad at me. "You know better than that!"

"I didn't mean to," I said. And it was true, it had just kind of happened. I thought I should try to change the subject. "Who was that, anyway?"

"She was a fortune-teller," Mom told me.

"She was?" I said. I shouldn't have been surprised, but I was. I thought fortune-tellers would look the way they were described in my books at home — long, colorful skirts; crystal balls and gold earrings; maybe even a turban. I turned my head for a quick look back. In her plain, yellow shirt, sitting in her chair, she still looked more like Melody's mom than a fortune-teller.

"Yes," Mom said. "She tricked us into having your fortune

told. By the time Grandma and I saw you with her, she had already started, so we had to let her finish."

"She did?" I said. I didn't really feel that bad about getting tricked. I was more excited about my fortune. I'd never had my fortune told before. "What was my fortune? What did she say?"

"Oh, I don't know," Mom said, trying to wave me off. "Something about how the lines on your fingers are a circle, so it means you have a special skill you'll always use."

"Really?" I said. I did a hopping step as we exited the tunnel. "What else? What else?"

"She also said the shape of your fingers means you are sensitive and creative and live in your own world," Mom said, and laughed a little. "She said because of this, you are going to get into trouble, so she wanted to give you blessings to protect you."

If your fingerprint looks like this, it means you have a special skill.

If your fingertip is this shape, it means you are creative.

"Blessings?" I asked. "Was that what her singing was?"

"Yes." Mom nodded. "She said her blessings would help you. They would help keep you safe and happy."

I thought about my fortune. I was pretty sure I knew what

the special skill was that I'd use all my life. I knew my talent was writing and illustrating books. It had taken me a while to figure that out — three years ago, I had thought about it for a whole year. But now I knew, so I wasn't too worried about that. But I was worried about the trouble the fortune-teller thought I was going to get into. What kind of trouble? How would her blessings protect me? And for how long? Would her blessings run out?

"Why does Pacy get to have her fortune told?" Lissy said. "Can I get my fortune told, too?"

"Yes!" Ki-Ki said. "Me, too! I want my fortune, too!"

"No!" Mom said, shaking her head hard and walking faster toward Grandma's building. "It's just a lot of nonsense. We don't believe any of those things. Just forget it."

Lissy looked at me jealously. She made a disappointed face, and as she passed me to go up the stairs, she whispered, "Lucky!"

Was I? The more I thought about my fortune, the more I wasn't sure.

Chapter 9

The Garbage Truck

Auntie Jin giving garbage
to the garbage man

THE NEXT MORNING, MOM HAD TO SHAKE US AWAKE
again.

"Wake up! Wake up!" she said. We all groaned, and Ki-Ki
tried to push her hands away.

"It's early!" I moaned.

"Not very early," Mom said, "but early enough. You have
your art classes today!"

"I don't care," Lissy mumbled, turning over. I did the same
thing.

Somehow, Mom got us all out of bed, but I felt like I was
sleepwalking. Lissy bumped my arm while we were brushing
our teeth, and I nudged her back. She elbowed me, and it
would've turned into a fight except Mom came in with Ki-Ki
to wash her face. Still, I stepped on Lissy's foot on the way
out the door. I was very grumpy.

And slow. I felt like a turtle caught in a puddle of honey. Mom had to push me to the table, and none of us smiled a morning greeting to Grandma, Grandpa, and Dad or even to Auntie Jin, who was at the stove heating something.

"Jet lag, still," Grandma, nodding, said to us.

Mom had said jet lag was when your body was confused, but I didn't feel confused at all. Instead, I felt like an irritated mosquito bite. In fact, I was certain that I was very, very grumpy.

"How many days until we go back home?" I asked, grumbling.

"We've been here for only two days!" Dad said. "You still have twenty-six days to go. Are you ready to leave so soon?"

"It's important you get to know Taiwan better," Mom said. "You'll learn about our culture. It's a part of who we are."

"I don't want to know who I am, then," I said rudely.

"Pacy!" Mom said in a shocked voice. Lissy and Ki-Ki looked at me sideways, and I shrank a little in my chair.

"Never mind, never mind," Auntie Jin said, interrupting us and coming over with a big platter. "Eat. You will feel better after you eat."

Things that looked like long, golden-fried hot-dog buns were on the platter. When Auntie Jin put one on a plate in front of me, I jabbed at it with my fingers. I didn't want to end up eating something weird again, like the chicken feet.

"What is this?" Lissy said. She was probably thinking about the chicken feet, too.

"It's called *youtiao*," Mom said. "It's kind of like a donut. You'll like it."

"Are there any Lucky Charms?" Ki-Ki asked. That was our favorite cereal at home. It had hard, sweet marshmallows in it that tasted like candy.

"We'll get some later," Mom said. "Today, eat this."

I rolled it back and forth on my plate like a rolling pin. "I'm not hungry anyway," I said.

Auntie Jin came back to the table with big cups of warm soy milk, the steam drifting from them like disappearing ghosts. "Try it with this," she said. "Dip it in the milk and eat. It'll taste good."

I watched Ki-Ki dip half a *youtiao* into a cup of soy milk and rip at it with her teeth. I picked up my piece.

Then, just when I was about to dip it in the milk, we all suddenly heard a noise outside. No, not a noise — a song! A

youtiao and
warm soy milk

chiming, jolly song was playing out on the street. Ki-Ki, Lissy, and I looked at one another in amazement. We knew that song! It was the ice-cream truck song!

"Aiya!" Auntie Jin said, and without another word, she jumped up and rushed out the door. Lissy, Ki-Ki, and I followed her. Was Auntie Jin going to get some ice cream? As we hurried, the ringing song got louder and louder, sounding like a music box with a microphone. I jumped down the stairs two at a time, and Ki-Ki kept chirping "Wait for me! Wait for me!" like a repeating bird. None of us wanted to miss the ice-cream truck. I hoped they had the chocolate-dipped ice-cream cones—the ones where the ice-cream man dipped the soft, white ice cream into a fudge sauce that hardened into a thin, delicious chocolate coating as it was handed to you. Those were my favorite. Would they have them here in Taiwan? Even so early in the morning? Maybe people in Taiwan always had ice cream at breakfast time.

my favorite
ice-cream cone

So, when we finally got to the street, it was a shock to see Auntie Jin dragging a trash bag over to a big, stinky garbage truck! There was no ice-cream truck anywhere. Auntie Jin waved to the garbageman as the garbage truck drove away, playing the jingly music that echoed through the streets. As Auntie Jin turned, we stared at her and the truck with our mouths open.

"What's wrong?" she asked us.

"Where's the ice cream?" Ki-Ki said.

"What ice cream?" Auntie Jin said, looking around, confused.

Lissy was the first one to get over our shock.

"There's no ice cream," Lissy said, and then explained to Auntie Jin, "In the United States, the ice-cream truck plays that song."

"Ice-cream truck?" Auntie Jin said. "What's that?"

"It's a truck that goes around and sells ice cream. It plays music, the same song, just like that," I said, motioning to the leaving garbage truck, "so everyone knows they can come out and buy ice cream."

"Ah," Auntie Jin said, nodding. "Here, the garbage truck plays that music so everyone knows they can come out and throw away their garbage!"

With that, Lissy, Ki-Ki, and I looked at one another. For a moment, we didn't say anything, because we were so embarrassed. But then Lissy let out a snort. "Garbage!" she said. "We came out for garbage!" And we all started to giggle. It was silly. We had run all the way for ice cream, and instead it was garbage! We laughed back up the stairs to our breakfasts, and our jet lag bad moods flew away like airplanes through the clouds.

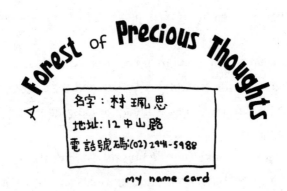

Chapter 10

名字: 林 珮 思

地址: 12 中山路

電 話 號 碼: (02) 2941-5988

my name card

AFTER BREAKFAST, MOM GAVE US EACH A NAME CARD.

"Put this in your bag or your pocket," she told us. "I want you to carry it with you all the time, so if you get lost, you can always give that to someone who can bring you back."

I looked at it. All the writing on it was in Chinese, a mix of symbols that I couldn't understand. I knew that the first line was my name—those characters were familiar. Mom had shown me my Chinese name a long time ago. But I had never thought about it as symbols meaning something the way Dad had talked about at the art store. It was strange to think these symbols that I couldn't read were supposed to mean me.

"Lin..." I said as I drew my fingers over the characters. "Pacy."

"No," Mom said. "It says *Lin Pai-se*. See, there are three

characters, one for *lin*, one for *pai*, and one for *se*. We made
Pacy a nickname from *Pai-se*."

林 = LIN, my last name in Chinese

木 = tree   林 = forest

my name in Chinese =

林　珮　思

LIN　　PAI　　SE
(Lin　Pacy)

"What's mine, then?" Ki-Ki asked.

"Lin Kai-se," Mom told her. "*Ki-Ki* is a nickname from
Kai-se. The word *se* means 'thought.' *Kai* means 'victorious,'
so your name, Kai-se, means 'victorious thought.'"

"What does *Pai-se* mean, then?" I asked.

"See the symbol for *Pai*? It is similar to the character for
jade," Mom said. "So your name means 'precious' or 'treasured thought.'"

"What does Lissy's name mean?" Ki-Ki asked.

"*Lissy* is a nickname from *Li-se*, which means 'beautiful
thought,'" Mom told us. I made a face. I didn't think Lissy

was a beautiful thought at all. They should have called her "bossy thought" — that would've been better.

"*Lin* means 'forest,'" Mom continued. "See how *Lin* is made up of two of the same symbols? Each means 'tree.' So when you put two 'trees' together, it means 'forest.' So *Lin* means 'forest' or 'woods.'"

Pacy. Pai-se. Precious thought. Lin. Forest.

That made me feel strange. I didn't feel like a precious thought, much less a forest of them. Still, I liked the idea. I could imagine it like something out of a fairy tale where precious thoughts, glittering and glistening, grew from diamond trees. Maybe I could paint that idea with a white horse in class.

painting Class

my strange first
bamboo painting

THE BUILDING THAT AUNTIE JIN TOOK US TO DIDN'T look like a place that would have painting classes. It was just a building, almost like a hospital. We had to ride an elevator to get to the floors of our classrooms. Ki-Ki's class was in the basement, so Mom brought her there, and Auntie Jin brought me and Lissy to our classes.

We were late when we got to my classroom. Now that I was awake, I wished I hadn't taken so long to get up. Everyone stared at me as I came in, and I stared right back. All of a sudden, a heavy, hard feeling filled my stomach as if I had swallowed a stone.

It felt just like that Taiwanese-American convention. Everyone in this class was Asian, just like in the class I had taken there. At home in New Hartford, Lissy, Ki-Ki, and I were the only Asian girls. When I was in first grade, a mean bus driver asked me where I was from and got angry with me when I said I was from up the street. "No," he had said. "Where are you *really* from?" He had made me cry. I had cried at that convention, too.

But I wasn't going to cry here. *Stop it,* I told myself. *Maybe it won't be like that.*

Auntie Jin talked to the teacher, a man in a black T-shirt who was older than Dad but younger than Grandpa. Most of the back of his head was bald, but he had some hair brushed over, like thin wisps of gray smoke. When he smiled a greeting at me, I could see his teeth were yellow. I sat down in the nearest empty seat.

"Okay," the teacher said as Auntie Jin left. "Back to what I was saying. Chinese painting is not about a picture; it is about telling a message. Each object in the painting has a special meaning. So we don't look at a Chinese painting; we *read* a Chinese painting."

He spoke English slowly and with a thick accent. His English was kind of like Mom's and Auntie Jin's, but it was harder to understand him. Or maybe it was

the painting teacher

what he was talking about that was so hard for me to understand. Read a painting?

He kept talking and holding up pictures in books while I looked around the room. The other students already had their paintbrushes and paints neatly on their desks. As quietly as I could, I started to take out the art supplies from the bag Mom had given me. I wondered what the teacher's name was. I guessed I had missed the part where he introduced himself. As I shifted the thick roll of paper that was still in my bag, things rolled around the bottom like marbles. I peered in. Color paint tubes! Bright rose red, golden yellow, leaf green, and blue in small tubes, like little traveling toothpastes, just for me. I had never had paints in tubes before — at school the paint always came in shared jars or in flat colored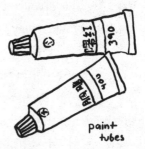

paint tubes

disks you added water to. Suddenly I felt better about the class. At least I would get to paint like a real artist.

"Chinese artists paint flowers together that do not grow together in real life," the teacher continued. He stumbled over some of his words, sometimes repeating them. "It is more about the idea or memory of the flowers or birds or the bamboo — not what it actually looks like. We have the idea of bamboo, and we paint the idea."

I didn't know if the teacher was going to be that good. He

seemed kind of awkward and kept bumbling. I couldn't imagine him as an artist. I glanced around the room. Most of the students were looking blankly at the teacher. One boy was scratching his leg, and a girl was looking out the window. Whether or not he was a good artist, the teacher was definitely dull. No one seemed to be having any ideas about bamboo.

The girl next to me looked at me, as if studying me. Her hair touched her chin, and she had glasses with gold wire frames. She didn't seem very friendly. There was no way she could tell I was a Twinkie yet, was there? I wondered if being a Twinkie showed up in the way I walked or on my face. I quickly looked away.

On her desk was a piece of black felt with AUDREY CHIANG written in a corner in perfect white letters. That must've been her name, and I wondered how she was able to get her name to show on the black cloth. Had she used white paint? I unfolded and laid out my piece of black felt, placed my paintbrushes on the side, and took out my paper.

on Audrey's desk

Then, unexpectedly, everyone stood up. The teacher was motioning all of us to come around his desk. We watched as he squeezed drops of black ink into his small bowl, mixed the ink and the water with his paintbrush, and then, with just a few strokes and movements of his hand, painted a stalk of bamboo with blowing leaves on the paper. It looked easy. I hoped he would show us harder things, too.

"You do not erase in Chinese painting. You cannot take back anything you do," said the teacher in his hesitating way. He painted more bamboo leaves. "The only way you can change your picture is with your next stroke, your next motion. It will take a lot of practice before you will be able to do a painting for our exhibit at the end of the summer. First, we paint bamboo."

He sent us back to our desks. What was that about an exhibit? I must have missed something else, too. But now we were painting bamboo. That was disappointing. It seemed so dull and boring. And it was just black ink, no colors. I was hoping to open those tubes.

the right way to hold a Chinese paintbrush

But painting bamboo wasn't easy! The ink had a sneaky way of swelling on the paper, making careful lines into blobs. And holding the paintbrush was tricky. The teacher kept pushing my arm. "Wrist up!" he said, shaking his head when I let my hand rest on the table. He shook his head again and pointed at the painting. "Try again," he said to me before moving on. "Think about the idea of the bamboo. Only the bamboo."

I tried to think about the bamboo, but the watery ink and the paintbrush seemed to have their own ideas. Strokes spread and bent in directions I didn't want, and I couldn't erase them or cover them up. A shock went through me. I had thought my special art skill was going to make it easy and my painting would be the best in the class. But my painting didn't even look like bamboo. Instead, it looked like strange, sickly gray sausage. Where was my art talent?

I stole a look at Audrey Chiang. She was concentrating hard on her painting, flicking her wrist to make a jointed bamboo stalk. I was glad to see that her painting was even worse than mine. Her bamboo looked like dark storm clouds.

And, actually, so did her face. She saw me looking at her painting and scowled.

"Anyway, it's not like painting counts or anything," she said. She was looking at her painting, so I wasn't sure whom she was talking to.

Still, just in case, I said, "What?"

"This class is just extracurricular," she said, now looking at me. "We don't get grades, so if I don't do well, it won't go on my record."

"Oh," I said. I didn't really understand what she was talking about, but I felt surprised and relieved at the same time, as if I had caught a falling glass ornament without breaking it.

Maybe she hadn't been thinking about my being a Twinkie. She seemed to have been spending a lot of time thinking about something else. Audrey noticed my confusion.

"I know you don't get grades for the summer geometry and science classes, either," she said. "But those make sure that you get A's during the school year, and that counts."

Audrey was only making me more confused. The only summer math class I had heard of in New Hartford was if you failed something and had to make up for it. But Audrey was definitely talking about something else. A summer class so that you get A's? It must be so when you took the class again in school, it would be easier. Taking a class twice made sense if you were doing it just to get a good grade. But I thought it was kind of weird.

"I don't take summer math classes," I said to her.

"You don't?" she said. Obviously, it wasn't weird to her at all. But the way she was talking about it was making me uncomfortable. Her words were shooting over each other like fast flying bullets. It made me feel like I was being attacked. "How do you make sure you stay the best in your class, then?" she said.

"I'm not," I said. Maybe I should have lied. But it was my worst subject.

"Oh," Audrey said, and her eyebrows went up over the rims of her glasses. If she hadn't been thinking I was a Twinkie before, she was definitely thinking something like

69

that now. She looked at me like I was a dog that had been hit by a car, half-pitying and half-disgusted. Then, as if I had faded away into worthlessness, her eyebrows went back down, and she turned back to her painting. The sinking feeling came back inside me.

I squeezed more ink into my bowl and watched black drops balloon like evil genies. I wished I wasn't here. I wished we hadn't come to Taiwan. I wished I was home. How many days until I could go back home? Twenty-six days. These were going to be the longest twenty-six days of my life.

the masterpiece dish of
sushi and sashimi

FOR DINNER THAT NIGHT, A FRIEND OF DAD'S WAS taking us to a Japanese restaurant.

"Japanese food?" Lissy asked. There wasn't a Japanese restaurant in New Hartford, so we had never eaten Japanese food before. "Isn't that, like, sushi and raw fish? Are we going to eat raw fish?"

"I hope so!" Dad said. "You know, Taiwan has a mix of Chinese and Japanese culture, so the Japanese food is very good here."

"But raw fish!" I said. Ki-Ki and I wrinkled our noses, but Lissy's face took on a look of daring. I could tell she was thinking of bragging to her friends at home about how she ate raw fish.

"You should try it!" Dad said. "And I bet this restaurant will have the best!"

It was a fancy restaurant. I was glad I wore my nicest dress, the one with the strawberries on it. All the waiters were dressed in suits, and we could see chefs dressed in black with black hats behind a glass wall. Ki-Ki's shoes squeaked on the floor.

me in my favorite strawberry dress

Dad's friend smiled at us. "I ordered for us already," he told us. "But if you want something special, let me know."

I didn't know what there was to ask for, but I said hopefully, "Dumplings?"

"Pacy!" Lissy groaned and rolled her eyes as Mom and Dad laughed and said something in Taiwanese to Dad's friend and his wife. I shrugged. Maybe they didn't have dumplings in Japan.

"How do you like Taiwan?" Dad's friend's wife asked us.

"It's nice," Lissy said, answering for all of us. "It kind of feels like Chinatown in New York City."

"That's because we've only been in Taipei so far," Mom said, and then to Dad's friend, "Next week we're going to go to Taichung."

"Ah, Taichung!" Dad's friend said. "Better be careful traveling during Ghost Month!"

The Ghost Month again!

"Why?" I asked.

"Ah, don't you know?" he said, with a teasing look in his eyes. "Some ghosts want to make you into one! During Ghost Month, if you aren't careful, they can come and erase you away!"

We laughed because we knew he wasn't serious. But the idea of getting erased gave me a shiver. Mom had said that people thought hungry ghosts could make trouble, and the fortune-teller had said that my fingers had told her that I would get into trouble. Was I going to get into ghost trouble? Could I be erased?

A waiter came by with metal tongs and handed each of us a warm, moist white towel, taking my mind away from ghosts. As I rubbed my hands in it, I was embarrassed to see that my fingers left gray streaks on the snowy fabric. I quickly folded it over.

"I thought a Japanese restaurant was supposed to have those bamboo mats," Lissy said, "and make you kneel on cushions on the floor to eat."

I didn't know how Lissy knew about Japanese things, but in one of my favorite books at home, *Miss Happiness and Miss Flower*, a girl made a Japanese dollhouse with bamboo floor mats and a low wooden table. I looked around the room. Everyone had white stone tables and black leather chairs like we did. The only thing bamboo was a plant in the corner.

"Maybe that's only when you are in Japan," I said to Lissy. "Maybe this is a Taiwanese-style Japanese restaurant."

"I think we are getting cheated," she hissed at me behind Mom's back. I shrugged.

But we were definitely getting real Japanese food. As soon as the waiter took away the towels, he put an odd-shaped, shallow black bowl in front of each of us. A mossy-green soft mound lay nearest to me, like a lump of clay waiting to be molded. But beyond that, on top of crystals of ice, cool pink rectangles lay fanned out against one another with a squid head peeking out from behind. I didn't need anyone to tell me what they were. I knew they were the raw fish!

raw fish

Lissy's eyes took on a bold look, and she swooped into her bowl with her chopsticks and put one of the pink pieces in her mouth. Ki-Ki and I looked at each other. We couldn't let Lissy be braver than us! I took a big gulp of air, reached with my chopsticks (holding them the wrong way, of course), took a piece of raw fish, and chewed.

And it wasn't too bad. It wasn't slimy, as I'd expected it to be. The fish was cool and tender in my mouth and slipped down my throat easily. I swallowed proudly.

"Your kids can eat sashimi," Dad's friend said. "Good for them!"

"It's their first time," Dad said, looking at us, pleased.

"Try it with this," Mom said, nudging an eggcuplike bowl full of soy sauce at us.

I dipped another piece of fish into the soy sauce and took a bite. The salty soy sauce with the soft fish tasted...good! Maybe I actually liked eating raw fish?

"Is this mashed peas?" I asked, poking at the mound of green stuff. It seemed more like green mashed potatoes, though.

wasabi

"No," Dad said. "It's wasabi. You can mix it in the soy sauce. It gives the sauce a spicy flavor."

Lissy took a big chunk from her plate and dumped it into the soy sauce. She mixed it with her chopsticks, and the wasabi swirled into the soy sauce, making it the color of a dirty puddle after a rainstorm.

But I wasn't afraid. So far, eating raw fish had been easy. I plopped my third piece of fish into the muddy mixture and bit it without waiting.

Ooowww! The flavors burned up through my mouth into my nose as if I had sneezed the sun, and my eyes started to tingle with tears. I spit the fish out on my plate, not caring that it was rude. I stuck my tongue straight out of my mouth, hoping that the air would put out the fire running through my face. I grabbed my cup of tea and poured it into my mouth.

It was only after I'd swallowed the tea that I realized everyone at the table was laughing at me.

"I guess you don't like it," Dad told me. "Wasabi does have a very strong flavor."

"Pain is not a flavor!" I said hotly.

Luckily, the waiter showed up and placed new dishes in front of us, and everyone forgot about laughing at me. This new plate had a big bright-orange crab sitting on it like a majestic king, its round eyes staring at me coldly.

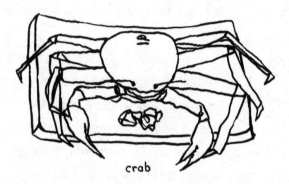

crab

"Yum!" Lissy said, attacking the crab and ripping off one of the legs savagely. She plucked the delicate snow-white meat popping from the leg shell with her chopstick and closed her eyes as she swallowed. Ki-Ki whined about not being able to eat her crab, so Mom helped her crack the shells. I liked crab, but the fiery flavor of the wasabi was still in my mouth, so I just drank tea, hoping the burning would leave.

And I kept drinking tea. Cup after cup, during the next dish—a bowl of thin-sliced meat in a souplike sauce—and when the main dish, the one Dad called "the masterpiece,"

teapot with tea

was served. It was a huge platter with a blue glass bowl of raw fish on ice, but this time pieces of fish were coral orange and reddish purple. Against a fan of brown twigs, a rainbow-glowing pillar rose from the bowl, holding two large pieces of pale pink fish (later Lissy took it out and saw there was an electric light inside). Pieces of sushi—black seaweed-rolled rice with bright patterned centers that looked like they were slices of a kaleidoscope—were arranged around the bowl on the plate so that the whole thing looked like an exotic floral arrangement. There were a lot of "oohs!" and "aahs!" when the waiter brought it out, and not just from our table.

By that time, I had drunk so much tea that I had to go to the bathroom. Everyone was so busy eating that no one noticed when I got up to go to the restroom in the back of the restaurant.

Like the restaurant, the bathroom was also very fancy. Everything was shiny and white, except for the floor—which was a soft-gray stone. It was a one-person bathroom, and as soon as I locked the door, I could make faces at myself in the big mirror that lined the whole wall.

But when it was time to flush the toilet, I was confused. There wasn't a silver lever to flush, like what I was used to.

Instead, there were all these buttons! I counted twelve of them and each one was labeled — but the labels were in Chinese! I couldn't read any of them!

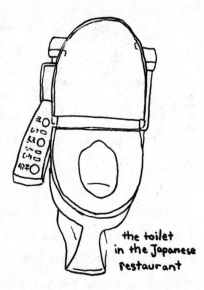

the toilet in the Japanese restaurant

I wasn't sure what to do. Why did they need so many buttons? What did all those buttons do? I was kind of scared to find out — maybe something really gross would happen and the water would come shooting out. Ew! But I didn't want to not flush the toilet, either.

I stared at the buttons. None of the symbols looked even a little familiar. Most of the buttons were gray circles, but there was a square yellow button and a red button. I tried to think. They would make the one that was most used the most noticeable, right? So it was probably the red or the yellow one. But which? I reached out my finger and pushed the red button.

Beep! Beeep! Beeeeep! A screeching noise like a fire engine filled the room. I covered my ears. Oh no! I had hit the wrong button!

Underneath the screaming sirens, I could hear quick footsteps coming and a shout through the door. I didn't know what to do. I was going to get in trouble! I started to hit the other buttons to try to make the alarm stop. The toilet started to vibrate and even play music! If I hadn't been so scared about the alarm, I would've thought it was funny.

Then I heard a scraping at the door. I stood frozen as the door burst open and a crowd of waiters and the receptionist stared at me.

I looked at them with big eyes. "Sorry?" I offered. The receptionist, who was in the front, shook his head and said something to everyone else. The alarm stopped, and everyone began to leave. It was only then that I saw Mom, Dad, Lissy, and Ki-Ki standing there, looking puzzled and worried. They had been in the back of the crowd.

"What happened?" Ki-Ki asked.

"I didn't know which button to push to flush the toilet," I said.

"Which one did you push?" Lissy said.

"The red one," I said, pointing.

"The red one!" Lissy said, making a face at me. "Out of all the buttons to push! Haven't we watched enough of Ki-Ki's cartoons? The red button is always the trouble one! You never push the red button!"

Mom pushed the yellow button, and the toilet flushed. "It's a Japanese toilet," she said, laughing. "And a very fancy one with all kinds of luxuries — it can even play music!"

I already knew that. Everyone else went back to the table

79

as I washed my hands. I thought about what a bad day it had been. The ice-cream truck had turned out to be a garbage truck this morning, Audrey Chiang had made me feel bad, I had burned my mouth with wasabi, and now I had triggered the bathroom alarm!

I still felt embarrassed when I went back to the table. People were probably looking at me and thinking about how I was the one who'd pushed the red button. My face felt about as red as that button.

But when I sat down, Dad's friend smiled.

"They almost forgot," he said as he pushed a plate in front of me. "Gyoza, Japanese dumplings, for you!"

Five fried dumplings sat on the plate, like nuggets of gold. I grinned and grabbed at them with my chopsticks. Gyoza were a little different from jiaozi, the Chinese fried dumplings I was used to. The dumpling skin was thinner

gyoza
(Japanese dumplings)

and crispier. But they were still delicious.

"Feel better?" Mom asked me.

I nodded, my mouth full of food. There was no day that dumplings couldn't make better.

Chapter 13

Audrey Chiang looking
at my painting

GOING TO CLASS THE NEXT MORNING WAS JUST AS
hard as it was the first time. "Come on!" Mom said to me as I
stumbled out the door. "You're going to be late again!"

And I was late again. But it didn't matter — we were still
painting gray bamboo. Even though the ink was black, we
were supposed to mix it with water so that there could be
different shades of gray. We had to paint bamboo "with vari-
ation," which to me just meant painting bamboo over and
over again.

"What's so important about bamboo?" a girl asked. I was
pretty sure her name was Eva Wong. She had long hair that
went all the way down below her waist. She could sit on her
ponytail.

"Bamboo is a symbol for long life because it never loses its
leaves, even in winter," the teacher said. "Also the Chinese

word for *bamboo* sounds like the word *wish*. So if you want to wish someone something, you paint a picture of that something along with bamboo."

That wasn't really what Eva was asking, but we all kept painting. Or at least, tried to paint. It bothered me that I couldn't erase or even cover up any of the paint strokes I made. My art skill didn't seem to be working here in Taiwan. I was used to my talent making me a good artist, but one look at my paper told me I was not. It made me feel uneasy and worried, like part of me was vanishing.

So every time I lifted the brush, I was nervous. Whatever mark I made I was stuck with. It made me feel afraid to paint. Would this stroke be okay? Would I make a mistake?

I looked around at everyone else's paintings. No one's paintings were great, but some people were getting their strokes to actually look like bamboo. Eva and the boy sitting next to her (I thought his name was Rex, but I didn't know his last name) were even painting leaves.

The teacher saw me with my brush frozen above the paper. "Relax," he said, moving my hand. "Press down, stroke, press, stroke, press."

His fingers loosened my grip on the brush and the paint glided gracefully on the paper like a figure skater on ice. *Aah*, I thought. *That's how it's supposed to look.* Too bad the teacher couldn't hold my hand while I did the whole painting. I wondered if I would ever learn his name.

I couldn't ask Audrey Chiang. I didn't know if it was because she thought I was a Twinkie, but she was not very friendly. She wasn't exactly mean, though, either. She wasn't making fun of me or whispering bad things. It was more like she looked at me as if I were a red light in a traffic jam.

I tried not to think about her. *Think bamboo*, I told myself as I painted. *Bamboo*. And slowly, as the class went on, my brush began to get the message. Even though I still made more mistake marks than good ones, my paintings were starting to get better. My bamboo stopped looking like gray hot dogs sprouting fat fingers and began to look a bit like bamboo. I let out a deep breath. Maybe my spe-

my bamboo
painting

cial art skill hadn't left me. But it was really hard to make it come out. At least I was getting better, though.

Audrey's paintings were getting better, too. The lumpy

Audrey's bamboo
painting

gray cotton balls she had been painting were now bamboo stalks arching across the paper. I had to admit her paintings were good. She obviously knew it, too, because her face was no longer scowling but had a look of smug contentment. She reminded me of Lissy when Mom let her choose her TV show.

The teacher walked by and stopped between us.

"Good! Good!" he said to me. "This is a nice line here."

"Isn't that the line you helped her with?" Audrey shot out. Before I could shake my head—because it wasn't the line he had helped me with!—she said, "And everything is one shade. You said our paintings should have variations of gray."

"Ah, yes," the teacher said to me as my eyes burned at Audrey. "Remember, even though we are using only black, the painting should have shade variations. It gives the bamboo more depth. Like here."

He was pointing at parts of Audrey's paintings, and even though I was looking, I wasn't paying attention. Inside, I was seething like a teapot about to whistle. Anger was bubbling inside me, and I clamped my mouth tightly to keep it from exploding. As I watched Audrey's face settle back into self-satisfaction, all I wanted to do was slap her. Why had she done that? Why would she point out what was wrong with my painting? "How do you make sure you stay the best in your class, then?" she had asked me. This must be the way she made sure she stayed the best in the class.

I rubbed my paintbrush in the ink violently. Blackness splattered on my fingers, staining me with evil-looking freckles. All my worries and fears about my art talent dissolved with my anger. Audrey Chiang wanted to be the best? Well, I had a special art skill. I'd make it come out, and I'd be just as good as she was. No, I would be better.

I took out another sheet of paper to start a new bamboo painting. *Think bamboo,* I told myself. The teacher had said that *bamboo* means "to wish." I gripped my paintbrush. *With this bamboo,* I thought with eyes narrowing, *I wish to be better than Audrey Chiang.*

Chapter 14

Lissy sprawled on the couch acting dramatically

LISSY WASN'T LIKING HER CLASS, EITHER. "WE SPEND most of the time just mixing ink," Lissy said as we walked back to our grandparents' place. She didn't use ink from a bottle like I did; she had to use the inkstone and ink stick—wetting the stick with water and grinding it into the stone to make a dark charcoal color. "It's complete misery!"

inkstone & ink stick

Dad laughed when he saw our glum faces. "It's not so bad, is it?" he asked.

Ki-Ki laughed, too, even though nothing was funny. Ki-Ki wasn't minding her classes. She liked cutting paper and didn't even mind that tiny bits of paper fell off her like snowflakes when she left class. I rolled

Ki-Ki cutting paper

my eyes at her. I liked how Lissy was miserable better. I was glad someone else felt like I did, especially when Lissy threw herself on the couch and sprawled her arms dramatically. "Yes, it is!" Lissy said, closing her eyes as if she couldn't bear to see the world. "I can't believe I'm spending my summer rubbing a stone!"

Mom and Grandma followed us into the room.

"You aren't going to be spending the whole summer mixing ink," Mom said. "In fact, Grandma has a surprise for you today that I know you'll like."

"Birthday present." Grandma nodded.

"Lissy's birthday was in June," Ki-Ki said.

"A late birthday present," Mom said. "It's something many girls do here when they are teenagers, though usually an older teenager than you. But since we're in Taiwan now, I said it was okay...."

"What is it?" Lissy interrupted. She stopped flailing on the couch and sat up, excited.

"Grandma's going to take you to get photos done," Mom said.

"Photos?" I said. "Dad could take them right here."

"No, no," Mom said. "These are special photos. They dress

87

you up like a movie star or a princess or a bride and do your hair and makeup. Girls here love it."

Lissy was starting to get excited, especially when Mom mentioned makeup. Mom never let Lissy wear makeup at home.

"So it's like a model shoot?" Lissy said. "Will I be in a magazine or something?"

"No, but we'll get you an album of your photos for you to keep," Mom said.

"Just Lissy?" I asked. I wanted to get dressed up like a princess. "Can I do it, too?"

"Me, too!" Ki-Ki said. I didn't think Ki-Ki really knew what we were talking about, but she never wanted to be left out.

"This time, just Lissy," Mom said. "It's her late birthday present from Grandma. And anyway, like I said, even Lissy is a little young for it. But you can come watch if you want. Then you can see if you want it done the next time we come to Taiwan."

The next time we come to Taiwan? I thought. So far, this first time hadn't been that much fun. I hoped the next time would be when I was much, much older.

And watching didn't sound like that much fun, either. Dad was going to go to the store, so I thought maybe I'd go with him and Ki-Ki to buy Lucky Charms instead, but Lissy said, "You're going to come with me, right, Pacy?"

"I don't know," I said. "It'll probably be boring for me."

"You should come!" she said. "It won't be bad!"

"I don't know." I shrugged.

"Please," Lissy said. "It'll be more fun if you come."

I was astonished. Lissy never wanted me to go anywhere with her in New Hartford. She was always embarrassed to be seen with me or Ki-Ki or Mom. And now she was saying it would be more fun if I went with her?

Lissy saw my amazement, came up close to me, and said in a low voice, "I don't want to go by myself."

Suddenly, I understood. Lissy felt like I did! She didn't say it, exactly, but I knew she meant that the crushing crowds, the flying Taiwanese words, and the depressing painting classes made her feel uneasy and nervous, too. A warm feeling wrapped around me, and I felt like reaching toward her with a hug. Instead, I nodded.

"Okay," I said. "I'll come."

Lissy looked relieved. And I felt good. One of my teachers in New Hartford had taught me the saying "Misery loves company," and I realized that was true of a lot of things, not just misery. Sometimes, sisters loved company, too — at least they liked it in Taiwan.

Lissy's Photo Shoot

makeup
at the photographer's
studio

THE PHOTO STUDIO WAS ON THE TENTH FLOOR OF AN
old building. It wasn't so old that it didn't have an elevator,
but the elevator felt rickety. I was glad when we got to the
right floor. But as we went through the glass doors, I saw that
everything was shiny and new and polished like it had all
just come out of a magazine.

"Ni hao, Ni hao," a woman at the desk said. That meant
"hello"—I knew enough Chinese to know that. Grandma
spoke to her for a little while and then pointed at Lissy. The
woman smiled and then beckoned Lissy to follow her to another room. Lissy followed the woman, and then we followed
Lissy, like a parade.

In the other room were a counter and a whole wall lined
with mirrors. The counter was covered with all kinds of
makeup—little tubes of pink and red lipstick, black and gray

pencils, beige powders, and tubs of shimmery brown and blue eye shadow. It was as if someone had bought every-thing in the cosmetics aisle in our local pharmacy. Bright lightbulbs framed the mirror, and another wall was hidden by racks of hanging clothes, silky and colorful. It was just like a dressing room for a movie star. Lissy's face lit up as brightly as the lightbulbs.

The woman said something to Lissy, who looked at Mom to translate. "She said you should pick your clothes first," Mom told Lissy. "You can choose three different dresses."

That was fun. We all started looking at the dresses, push-ing through them as if we were trying to make waves in wa-ter. There were hundreds of pretty dresses, but Lissy was picky. "How about this one?" Mom would say. "This one?" Grandma would say. "No," Lissy would always reply, shaking her head.

Finally, Lissy chose two dresses and had only one more left to decide on. I thought Lissy had horrible taste in clothes. One dress was black with

Lissy and me looking at dresses

91

sequins sewn in the shape of a bow around the waist. The black skirt looked like it was made out of layers of nets and stuck out like an upside-down dandelion. Her other dress was red with rows of lace that made her look like a cross between a fire engine and a cake. I would've chosen one of the flowing chiffon dresses that had little diamonds sewn into it or at least the pink silk one with birds embroidered all over the top.

Lissy picks a dress

"Let Grandma choose your last dress," Mom said. "She's the one who's giving this to you."

Lissy nodded, and Grandma chose a Chinese dress the color of a blue butterfly. It was long and shiny and had a golden feathery pattern all over it. I could tell Lissy was disappointed, but she tried to hide it.

Now that Lissy was done choosing her dresses, another woman came in and had Lissy sit in the chair in front of the mirror. The woman looked at Lissy's dresses, took Lissy's chin in her hand, and then said something in Taiwanese to Grandma. Mom answered.

"What?" Lissy asked.

"She just wanted to know what kind of makeup you wanted," Mom said. "I told her the natural look."

Mom might have said the natural look, but what the woman was doing to Lissy was not looking that natural. The woman was brushing a beige color all over Lissy's face like she was painting a wall. Another woman appeared and began brushing and pulling and twisting at Lissy's hair. Lissy loved it. Ever since Lissy turned thirteen a year ago and said that she was officially a teenager because *teen* was at the end of her age, she rarely smiled. I guess she thought she was too old to show that she was happy. But now the corners of her mouth kept creeping up, and her cheeks, the parts that hadn't been painted beige, were blushing pink.

One of the women motioned for Lissy to close her eyes, and I was expecting her to put some eye shadow or something like that on Lissy, but she didn't. Instead, she measured Lissy's eyes with her fingers and then cut tiny slices out of a piece of clear sticker paper. Then she peeled the backing from her tiny shapes and carefully stuck them on Lissy's eyelids. What were those for?

Then the woman started smearing brown powder that looked like hot-cocoa mix on Lissy's eyelids, covering the stickers. She layered on more and more powder, some silvery, some charcoal gray, all the way up to Lissy's eyebrows. Those she plucked into clean arches, which made Lissy give

93

a little squeal with each pull. Ouch! Now I was glad I wasn't getting my photos done, too.

"Okay," she said to Lissy. She wasn't finished, but she meant that Lissy could open her eyes now.

"Eye folds!" Lissy said when she looked at herself. I was mesmerized. Our eyes were one of the biggest differences between us and our classmates in New Hartford. My friends Becky and Charlotte both had creases on their eyelids that made their eyes look round and big. My eyelids were smooth and heavy, which made my eyes look small. And slanted — the way they looked when the boys at school used to pull the corners of their eyes to make fun of me for being Asian. "Can you even see out of your eyes?" a boy once asked me.

But now Lissy's eyes looked big and round, almost like Becky's — though coated with a lot of makeup. I guess the woman needed to put that much on to hide the stickers. It was strange to see Lissy like that. With one woman dabbing pink onto Lissy's lips and another adding fake curls to the top of Lissy's head, Lissy wasn't looking much like Lissy anymore.

When Lissy came out of the dressing room in her black dress, her face looked like a mask of paint, and her hair was like a curled poodle on her head. She was smiling, though.

"I feel like a movie star!" Lissy said.

"You look like a movie star," Grandma said to her, and Lissy glowed like Christmas lights. But I didn't think she looked that good.

"They put too much makeup on you," I told her.

"In photograph, will look natural," the woman said. I guess she understood some English. I felt a little bad then. I didn't want her to think that I thought she did a bad job.

A man with a camera as large as a shoe box came into the room then to take Lissy to another room, where all the sets were.

"Better alone," he said to me in his broken English when I moved to follow them. "Person nervous when other people and bad photo. Alone, more relax."

That meant Mom, Grandma, and I stayed in the dressing room while Lissy got her photos done. That was boring. We could hear the clicking and snapping of the camera and the man's instructions. "Just small smile," he kept saying to her. "No big smile." I thought that should've been easy for her, but I guess this whole thing was making Lissy happy in a way that was unusual.

As Mom and Grandma talked, I looked at all the tubs of makeup and brushes and bottles that the women had used on Lissy. You needed a lot of stuff to look like a movie star. Some of the tubs on the counter reminded me of my ink and brushes in painting class. I wondered if Audrey Chiang thought she looked like a movie star. Probably not—she was full of herself, but she wasn't stupid.

I looked at myself in the mirror. I didn't really know if I was pretty. I knew I didn't look like a movie star, but

I did hope I was pretty. I didn't put my hair in barrettes anymore—I was too old for that. And Mom was letting me grow my hair long, and it was already a little past my shoulders. I wondered if I should grow it as long as Eva, that girl in my painting class, had grown hers. Her hair looked nice, though it probably took forever to comb. But even if I had really long hair like Eva's, I knew I'd never be really pretty, like my friend Charlotte in New Hartford was. Charlotte had wavy golden hair and blue eyes. Last year at my birthday party, Charlotte had said I wouldn't make a cute couple with Sam Mercer, the boy I liked in school. He had brown eyes and sand-colored hair. She had said I didn't match him, because I was Chinese. "It's hard to match you in a cute couple," she had said. "You don't fit anyone else."

I pulled up my eyelids to make my eyes bigger. If I had eye folds, would I be easier to match with Sam Mercer? In the fairy tale, Snow White had black hair, but she wasn't Chinese. Was it just my eyes that made me Asian? Being here in Taiwan, where I didn't know what the foods were, where I couldn't read the signs or even ask questions—I didn't feel Asian at all. Maybe eye folds would help me match who I was on the inside.

Chapter 16

Dad and his
new camera

LISSY WOULD HAVE TO WAIT TWO WEEKS BEFORE SHE could see her photos and then a week after that before she would get the album to keep.

"That's so long!" she said. I agreed. We'd be getting her album right before we left, and that was a long time from now, even though the days were passing a little faster.

But at least for now we were going to get a break from our classes. We were going to visit Taichung, where Dad's family lived, for about a week and stay with Big Uncle, Dad's oldest brother. Taichung was in the middle of Taiwan. It even *meant* "middle of Taiwan." "*Zhong* means 'middle,'" Dad said, "and *bei* means 'north' — *bei* is where the *pei* of *Taipei* comes from. *Zhong* is where the *chung* of *Taichung* comes from. So *Taipei* means 'north of Taiwan' and *Taichung* means 'middle of Taiwan.'"

Dad said we were taking the special bullet train that would get us there faster than the regular train. "They didn't have that when I was young," he said. I wondered if it was called a bullet train because it went faster than a speeding bullet—like Superman!

The train station was a huge building that I couldn't really look at because there were so many people. Ghost Month

train station

wasn't scaring many people from traveling, either, no matter what Dad's friend had said. Mom said we weren't going for very long, but she, Lissy, and Dad had rolling suitcases and Ki-Ki and I had heavy backpacks. Mom also carried a big shopping bag full of presents and her purse, and Lissy had another bag of gifts.

Around Dad's neck was what we thought was the worst

piece of extra luggage — a brand-new camera that he'd bought at a store down the street from our grandparents' place. It was supposed to take especially good photos, but, to us, it just took an especially long time to use. "Let me take a picture," Dad would say in the middle of whatever we were doing, and we would have to stand there forever while he figured out which buttons to press. Sometimes my face would get sore from holding the smile as he stood there trying to hit the right button for the right setting. I wondered if the camera was Japanese, like that toilet was.

Dad found out where we were supposed to be, and after more elbowing and squeezing, we found ourselves waiting on a platform. Lots of other people were waiting, too. I let my backpack drop to the ground, and Lissy sat on the suitcase she had been rolling behind her.

"I have to go to the bathroom!" Ki-Ki said.

"Really? Now?" Mom sighed.

Dad looked at the big clock. "There's time," he said. "You can go."

"Me, too!" I said. I didn't really have to go, but I thought it would be better to go with Mom to the bathroom than to try to go by myself later. I didn't want to push the wrong button again.

So Ki-Ki, Mom, and I shoved through the crowds again (it was a little easier this time without all our luggage) to the bathroom. It smelled bad.

"Here," Mom said, and she opened her purse and took out a blue change purse with gold embroidery. She handed it to me, brought me close, and whispered, "These are tissues. They don't have toilet paper in public bathrooms. Use this. Don't throw it down the toilet. There should be a garbage can in the corner, throw it there."

I nodded as Ki-Ki and Mom vanished into a stall. I went into the stall next to them but stopped. There was no toilet in there! There was a porcelain-covered hole in the floor. That was strange. It was kind of like a urinal but in the ground.

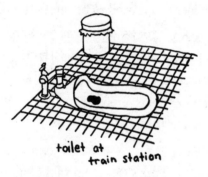

toilet at
train station

I didn't look that closely. Instead I went to the next stall and then the next. Same thing! Were we in the boys' bathroom? Or maybe someone had stolen the real toilets? And they couldn't afford to put a whole toilet in, so they just put in those? That didn't make sense. Why wouldn't they just have fewer stalls and put a whole toilet in each one?

By then, Ki-Ki had finished and I still hadn't found a toilet. As Mom and Ki-Ki left the stall, I saw there was a toilet in there, so I used that. That was the only toilet in the whole bathroom!

"Are we in the boys' bathroom?" I whispered to Mom as I washed my hands.

"What? No," Mom said. "Why?"

I nodded over at the stalls, and Mom laughed. "Those are a different kind of toilet. You're supposed to just squat over them."

It took me a little while to picture it, but once I did, I said, "*Ew!*"

Mom laughed again as I shook the water from my hands. "Those kinds of toilets were here before the ones you're used to. And most people like those better. See how there is only one Western toilet in the whole bathroom?"

"Why?" Ki-Ki asked.

"Well, people think they are cleaner," Mom said, motioning to a sign on the wall that I had missed before. It showed how to use (and not use) the bathroom.

sign on how to use (and not
use) the squat toilet

"They're not cleaner," I said. "Those toilets are in the ground!"

"They're cleaner for people using them," Mom said. She was laughing as she pushed us out the door. "Think about it. With these toilets, you don't have to worry about other people's butts."

We laughed, too, mainly because Mom said the word *butt*. And it felt better to think about that and laugh than to think about what she was saying. All this toilet talk was making me feel gross, and I was glad to leave it back with the bathroom.

apple candy

ALMOST IMMEDIATELY AFTER WE GOT BACK FROM THE bathroom, there was a thundering roar and the train came rushing in. As it screeched to a stop in front of us, the crowds buzzed and swarmed. Then the train doors slid open, and there was a great shove as people rushed through the doors like grains of salt through a funnel.

But as soon as we sat down and the train left the station, all was still. Not that the train wasn't moving — it was going fast. I watched out the window as the buildings passed faster and faster. But inside the train, everyone seemed like silent, sitting statues.

Dad fell asleep almost immediately. I guess he still had jet lag. Every once in a while, he would snore and we would all laugh.

Dad sleeping on train

"How do you say 'I can't speak Chinese' in Chinese?" Lissy asked Mom.

"*Wo bu hui shuo Hanyu,*" Mom said.

"Woo boo huwaay…" We all tried to repeat it, and the words tangled into a jumble. Ki-Ki and I giggled. Lissy shook her head.

"Too hard," she said. "I think one word at a time is better. What's the word for *bathroom*?"

"*Xishoujian,*" Mom said. "But in Taiwanese, it's *ben-so.*"

"Wait," I said. "There's a big difference? Chinese, Taiwanese — it seems the same to me!"

"You know," Lissy said, "Taiwanese is like slang."

"Not exactly," Mom said. "I guess Taiwanese is considered a dialect and Chinese the official language."

"What's a dialect?" Ki-Ki asked. This time, I was glad Ki-Ki was asking questions because I didn't know what a dialect was, either.

"Hmm…" Mom thought hard before she spoke. "If every state in the United States had its own language in addition to English, that language would be a dialect. In China, some areas have their own languages — their own dialects — but Mandarin Chinese is the official language everyone knows. When the Chinese took over Taiwan, they made Chinese the official language. But people still speak Taiwanese at home."

That was really confusing.

"So do people speak Chinese or Taiwanese here?" I asked.

"Well, Chinese is what people speak at work or at formal events," Mom said. "Chinese is more universal — the language that more of the world knows. But Taiwanese is what most people here speak at home with their friends or family. So we use both."

That meant all this time in Taiwan, people could've been speaking Chinese or Taiwanese to me and I would never have known. I sighed. It seemed hard to me, but Lissy wasn't discouraged.

"You'd better teach us Chinese, then," she said. "Then we can use it outside of Taiwan, too."

"Okay," Mom said. "In Chinese, the word for *bathroom* is *xishoujian.*"

"*Xishoujian,*" we all said together.

"What's the word for *please?*" Lissy asked.

"*Qing,*" Mom said.

"How about *sorry?*"

"*Duibuqi.*"

"*American?*"

"*Meiguoren.*"

A woman with a cart of snacks came by, and I was glad. My stomach had been rumbling the whole time. Mom

strawberry
Pocky

bought each of us some candy and a box of strawberry Pocky—which were kind of these long pretzels dipped in a strawberry coating. But it was sweet, not salty.

Mom wanted to teach us more Chinese words, but now we were more interested in our Pocky. I ate each pretzel one by one, scraping the pink strawberry layer with my teeth before crunching it, looking out the window the whole time.

After I finished my box of Pocky, I opened the bag of apple candy. It was good, but I was still hungry even after I ate the whole pack. I played with the wrapper, crinkling the Chinese words as I rolled it around in my hands. I wondered if the label just said *apple candy* or if the candy had a special name that meant something, like how *Pacy* meant "precious thought."

Thinking about my name reminded me of the name chops we were going to get carved. I still didn't feel much like a precious thought, so I wasn't sure if I wanted my name on it. I liked how some of Dad's friends had different things on their name chops. I didn't want "never too tired for knowledge," but "thoughts as evergreen as a pine tree" sounded kind of pretty. Like a piece of a poem. But the only poem I knew was the one that was on Valentine's Day cards: "Roses are red, violets are blue, sugar is sweet, and so are you."

burning money for
Ghost Month

And I wasn't going to put that on my name chop!

Outside the window, barrels burning bright flames for Ghost Month blurred by, and I thought about the ghosts visiting the living world. Maybe the ghosts felt the same way I did in visiting Taiwan. Here, everyone had conversations that flew through me, like I was steam from freshly cooked rice. Sometimes I felt as if no one even saw me, and that made me hollow and empty.

But maybe I just needed something to eat.

Chapter 18

Cousin Clifford

lady on
bicycle

WHEN WE GOT TO THE STATION, BIG UNCLE WASN'T there. Instead, beaming at us was Cousin Clifford!

"Surprise!" he said as he came up to us. "Are you happy to see me?"

We were. Ki-Ki and I ran over and jumped up and down, and Mom and Dad gave him a big hug. Even Lissy smiled. The last time we saw Clifford was when he got married in Boston, Massachusetts. Ki-Ki had been a flower girl, and I had jumped on his bed for good luck. He looked fatter and softer, but his grin was exactly the same. Seeing him made all my grumpiness from being hungry fall away like rain being shaken from a wet umbrella.

"We heard you were in Taiwan!" Mom said, even though she hadn't told us that. "Where's Lian?" Lian was Clifford's wife.

"She's at work," he said, grabbing one of the suitcases.

"Our company is probably going to keep us here for another year. Then we'll go back to the States."

"How long have you been here?" Dad asked.

"Since May," Clifford said. He put the suitcase down for a moment and started counting on his fingers. "So before this, I lived in Taiwan for two years. Now it's a total of two years and three months that I've lived here. But Lian says I still speak Taiwanese like a seven-year-old."

"What's wrong with that?" Ki-Ki asked, offended.

We followed Clifford out of the train station, and he spoke to us fast without a break. He said he was excited to speak in English to "native speakers" again. I kind of knew how he felt. Except for when I spoke with Lissy or Ki-Ki, speaking English here in Taiwan felt like work and made me feel impatient sometimes. In class, whenever the teacher spoke, it always took me a couple of seconds to understand what he was saying, as if I had to wait for an echo. Here, speaking English to almost everyone—Grandma, Grandpa, Aunt Bea, Uncle Flower, even Mom and Dad—was slower and clumsy.

"Sorry, you guys will have to take a taxi. Hope you don't mind," Clifford said. "I came on this."

"This" was a silver-gray motor scooter. It was a mix of a motorcycle and a bicycle—there was an engine and everything, but parts were covered by plastic, and there was a basket in the back. I liked it!

"Can I ride on it?" Lissy asked.

"Me, too! Me, too!" Ki-Ki and I echoed excitedly.

Mom shook her head at us. "I don't think it's safe for you," she said.

"It probably isn't." Clifford laughed, took a helmet out from the little carrier in the back, and began to strap it on his head. "People say they can tell that I'm from America because I use this helmet. Most people don't wear one. But I think that's crazy! The joke here is that traffic lights are not rules, just suggestions."

Clifford on a motor scooter

We saw what he meant as the taxi drove us to Big Uncle's place. It stopped and jerked and swayed, leaving angry honks behind us. Everything seemed confused, and the streets were small. One old lady was bicycling with boxes piled so high behind her that she looked like a moving mountain that took up a lot of room on the street. The taxi just squeezed past her, and as I worried that we might hit her, I saw a turtle's head stick out of one of the boxes. Most people were on motor scooters like Clifford's that swerved and sped around us like miniature rockets. There were a lot of motor scooters that had two, even three, kids clinging on to the driver.

Now I was kind of glad Mom hadn't let me ride on the motor scooter. In New York City and in Taipei, traffic had been really busy, but here in Taichung, it was a busy, fast-moving mess. In school, one of my vocabulary words was *chaos*, and for the first time, I felt as if I understood what that word meant. Even in the taxi, I didn't feel that safe.

chaos in
Taichung

"It's different here," I said. "I mean, different from Grandma's place."

"Yes, it'll be more..." Dad paused and then said, "I'm not sure how to say it in English. It will be more real Taiwan."

Real Taiwan? Weren't we already in real Taiwan? It was strange to hear Dad say that. How could it be more real? Was it like those dumplings that could tell if you were a real

Chinese person? Thinking about dumplings made me hungry. I didn't know if we were in real Taiwan, but I did know I was really hungry!

"There'll still be dumplings here, though, right?" I asked.

"Yes," Dad said in a voice that pretended to be annoyed, but I knew he was just joking. "There will still be dumplings! Don't worry! There will never *not* be dumplings anywhere in Taiwan."

I grinned.

niu rou mien
(beef noodles)

BIG UNCLE WASN'T BIG. HE WASN'T SHORT OR SMALL, but because everyone called him Big Uncle, I thought he was going to be really tall and strong. Instead, he was just a little taller and wider than Dad and had a red face with drooping, tired-looking eyes. But he did have a big smile, which welcomed us as we got out of the taxi.

He, Aunt Ami, and Clifford had been waiting for us, and almost before we were all out of the taxi, Clifford had unloaded our luggage. He took it inside up to Big Uncle's apartment and came back out.

Big Uncle

"What do you want for dinner?" Clifford asked as he led us down the street.

"Pacy wants dumplings!" Lissy and Ki-Ki said together. I was a little embarrassed, but everyone laughed.

"I know a good place close by that does beef noodles," Clifford said. "It probably has dumplings, too."

We followed Clifford across the street. Crossing the street was hard. I realized that if traffic lights were just suggestions for cars, then they were also just suggestions for people walking in the streets, too. I squinted my eyes shut and walked close to Clifford as cars honked and motor scooters swerved around us, but he and Big Uncle just walked without concern. They must've been used to all the confusion.

Clifford led us through a door to a small restaurant. The place was very plain with old but clean white tiles on the floor and five rough wooden rectangular tables with benches on either side. In the back was a small kitchen with a man standing over a huge steaming pot, like in the pictures of witches stirring their brew.

"*Ni hao, ni hao*," Clifford said to the man, who stuck his head out of the kitchen. Except for *ni hao*, I didn't understand the words Clifford said or what the man said back. But Mom and Dad looked pleased and ordered food with big smiles.

"What did he say?" I asked as we all sat down at one of the tables.

"They make *niu rou mien* here," Dad said, "special beef noodles – they are thicker than normal noodles and hand-pulled. They're very good! I haven't had real ones in a long time."

"What do you mean, 'real ones'?" I asked.

"The real good noodles are the ones that people make by hand. Come over here, and maybe you can see him make some," Dad said, motioning me over to his side of the table. Lissy, Ki-Ki, and I crowded beside him and stared.

The man was quickly rolling a big mound of dough. When it looked like a perfectly round white log, he took it and stretched it wide, as far as his arms could reach. Then, so fast that we could barely see what he was doing, he began to wave his arms back and forth, twisting and slapping the dough onto the counter in front of him. He seemed to whirl and whip the dough around like he was casting some sort of spell or enchantment. And maybe he was, because Lissy, Ki-Ki, and I didn't even notice that we'd walked closer to get a better look.

And it was magic, or close enough. Because, suddenly, in his hands were hundreds and hundreds of noodles. He had somehow stretched and pulled that roll of dough into long, perfect noodles – each one looking exactly the same. We were amazed.

He didn't think he had done anything that wonderful, though. He calmly took a pair of big scissors and cut the noodles into the waiting, steaming pot. As he stirred, he smiled at us, and we felt a little silly for staring at him with our mouths open. We went back to the table.

man making noodles

"He made noodles with his hands!" Ki-Ki said.

"Yes, I told you," Dad said. "Hand-pulled noodles. They're the best."

I wasn't sure if they were the best, but they looked pretty good. The bowls had big chunks of beef sticking up like mountains in a sea of savory brown soup filled with pale yellow noodles. The steam wafted, and my mouth watered as a bowl was put in front of everyone. Everyone except me, that is.

"Hey, where's mine?" I asked.

"Yours is coming," Mom said. "Have some of mine while you are waiting."

The hand-pulled noodles were good. Very good. Spicy and rich, the soup began to melt away the hungry ache in my stomach. But I wanted my own bowl. Where was mine?

"Here you go!" Clifford said as a different bowl was put in front of me. "We got this special for you."

I looked into the bowl. "Dumplings!" I said. "Wonton soup!"

"Not exactly," Clifford said. "You know, in America, what they call wontons is from a word in Cantonese, the dialect in Southern China."

"Really?" I said, but I wasn't that interested in what Clifford was saying. I was too busy eating.

"And if you translate the Cantonese word *wantan*, which *wonton* comes from," Clifford said, "it means 'swallowing clouds.' So you can consider eating a wonton like swallowing a cloud."

"Why?" Ki-Ki asked.

"Maybe because the wonton feels smooth when you swallow it," Clifford said. "Or maybe because of the shape — like clouds, no two wontons are exactly the same. Anyway, these dumplings aren't wontons. You can tell because they are in the shape of ears."

"Ears!" I said. I stopped eating for a moment. "What?"

STORY OF DUMPLING SOUP

Once there was a famous doctor, Zhang Zhongjing, who lived by the river in a cold part of China. He treated and cured many things, but in the winter, the things he treated the most were people's ears! That sounds strange, I know, but where he lived in China, the winters were particularly cold. The icy wind whipped and burned any exposed skin.

It was so cold that when a villager joked that his breath froze into pieces of ice in the air, all believed him because even if the cold did not freeze one's breath, it really did freeze people's ears. The doctor was kept busy during the winters treating frostbitten ears. He knew that people with frostbite needed warmth to heal, so he began to make a remedy that would warm people's insides as well as their outsides. He cooked meat with warming herbs and finely chopped it. Then he wrapped it in thinly rolled dough and boiled the pieces in soup with more herbs. When the mixture was finished, he called it "soup that takes away the cold," or "qu han jiao er tang." He then served it to his frostbitten patients, who not only healed quickly, but enjoyed the soup so much that they continued to eat it.

qu han jiao er tang
(Chinese dumpling soup)

People made the soup at home,

119

usually eating it in the winter. They say the dumpling is the shape that it is because it is made to resemble an ear, in honor of Dr. Zhongjing's treatment of people's frostbitten ears. The name of the soup, qu han jiao er tang, was shortened to jiao er tang, and the dumplings were eventually called jiaozi.

"*Jiaozi!*" I said. "I know that word! Dumplings! But we usually have them fried."

"Well, these are *jiaozi*, too." Clifford laughed and pointed at my bowl. "And they exist all because of frostbitten ears."

"How do you know all this?" I asked Clifford. I was impressed he was so smart.

"School, of course," he said as he began eating again.

"Did you go to cooking school?" Ki-Ki asked.

"No." He grinned between bites. "It was a Chinese culture appreciation course. But I really paid attention during the parts about the food."

Chapter 20

The **Market**

bag of frogs

WHEN WE CAME BACK FROM DINNER, LIAN WAS HOME from work, and there was more hugging and talking. More adults showed up — some were relatives and some were old friends. They all sat at the round table in Big Uncle's apartment, talking and talking in Taiwanese while Lissy, Ki-Ki, and I sat there bored and unimportant. At home, Mom was always so picky about when we went to sleep, but here she didn't say anything, even when the sky became as black as burnt incense. When I went to bed, everyone was still laughing around the table. I sighed. Mom had stopped noticing me, too.

And when I woke up the next morning, Aunt Ami, Mom, Dad, Big Uncle, Lian, and Clifford were still laughing and talking around the table. I knew they must have gone to sleep and woken up, because they were all wearing different clothes, but it felt as if nothing had changed.

"What are we doing today?" I asked.

"I'm not sure," Mom said, and handed me a bowl of rice porridge before turning back to the kitchen. "Dad thought we might go to the cemetery to see his parents' graves, but we're not sure yet."

I hoped Dad changed his mind. Going to a cemetery definitely did not seem like fun. Dad's parents died a long time ago; I never knew them. The only thing I did know of them was that two big black-and-white photos of them hung on the wall in the back corner of our living room. I tried not to look at them much, because they were serious, unsmiling portraits with grim eyes that seemed to look at me disapprovingly. Once, a long time ago, Lissy took down the photo of Dad's father, held it over her face, and chased me with it. She got in a lot of trouble.

"Aunt Ami doesn't want us to go to the cemetery," Clifford said.

"Why not?" Ki-Ki asked.

"Because it's Ghost Month," Clifford said, "and she thinks the only ones that would be at a cemetery now are hungry ghosts. Aunt Ami is very superstitious, you know. She won't even hang her laundry out to dry in the evenings."

"Why not?" Ki-Ki asked.

"Because ghosts might move into them!" Clifford said. We all laughed.

Our parents must have listened to Aunt Ami, because we didn't go to the cemetery. Instead, we went to the market. Going to the market was even harder than going to the noodle restaurant. We had to cross a couple of streets, and each time I felt like a car almost hit us. The streets seemed to get narrower and narrower and fuller, with more and more people. I had to step over planks of wood on the ground that covered holes in the road, garbage, and sleeping dogs. When I looked up, all I saw were layers of bright signs with Chinese words I couldn't read.

I wasn't sure when the street stopped being a street and turned into a market, but somewhere in the noisy, sticky

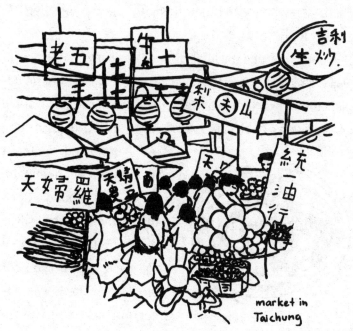

market in Taichung

crowd it had. Big umbrellas shaded the crates of fruit on display, and faded red paper lanterns lined the sky. Mom, Dad, Lian, Aunt Ami, and Big Uncle began to stop at different stalls and buy things.

"Clifford," Lian said, pointing at a display of some rosy, bell-shaped fruits, "your favorite!"

"Oh boy!" Clifford said, grinning. "Wax apples!"

Clifford began to fill a bag. "He can eat a whole bag in one day," Lian told us. "He is the super wax-apple eater."

wax apples

"You can't blame me! They're so good," he said, handing me, Lissy, and Ki-Ki one each. "And you can't get them in the States. Try it."

I took a bite, and the juice dripped down my chin. The fruit was crispy and sweet and so juicy! It was kind of like an apple, but not exactly. It was lighter and fresher—like an apple crossed with a bubble. I could see why Clifford loved them.

pot of eels

As I crunched, I almost walked into a big aluminum pot on the ground. Good thing I didn't! The silver pot was full of water and long black ropes. No, not ropes—eels! There was another pot next to it full of dark fish wavering in the water like captured shadows. Another pot had turtles, their small eyes looking at us like black stones, and next to all the pots was a mesh bag full of croaking frogs.

But I couldn't look at everything, because the person in charge of the stand said something in Chinese to me in an irritated tone. She seemed upset with me, probably because I almost stepped into her eels. I shook my head at her, and she said something louder. The skin of her round face was so tan that it was almost the same color as her eyes, which were flashing at me. I felt a little scared. A burning rushed through me. How did I say I couldn't speak Chinese, again? I couldn't remember. What were those words Mom had taught us on the train?

"*Meiguoren! Meiguoren!*" I said. That was the only word I could remember. *American*. She had the same look in her eyes as that mean bus driver in New Hartford from so long ago. "Where are you from?" he had asked me. My answer didn't satisfy her, either. She said something else to me, louder and louder, and all I could do was stare at her red-printed flowers on her apron, too frightened to look at her face. I knew she was angry, but I didn't know why. My cheeks burned red as if her words were slapping my face. "*Meiguoren! Meiguoren!*" I said again, stupidly — like a parrot. I didn't know what else to say. I felt like crying.

"What's up?" Clifford said, grabbing my arm. The woman

yelled something at him. "*Duibuqi, duibuqi,*" he said as he waved her away, and nudged me toward the road. "Sorry, sorry." I saw her shake her head in disapproval and disgust as Clifford dragged me away.

"She was mad at me!" I said to Clifford.

"She wasn't mad, exactly," he said. "She just didn't understand why you couldn't speak Chinese."

A heavy feeling fell upon me, like a crushing boulder. "Twinkie!" those girls at the Taiwanese-American convention had called me. "You lost your culture! Twinkie!" But I stuck my chin out.

"We don't speak Chinese in New Hartford," I said sullenly.

"I know," Clifford said. "Your parents wanted you guys to fit in there, so that's why they never taught you. But that woman didn't know that."

"I told her I was American," I insisted. "I said '*Meiguoren, Meiguoren*' over and over."

"She probably didn't know what you meant," Clifford said. "Here, people like us are called *Huaren*—'overseas Chinese.'"

"She knew what I meant," I said stubbornly. "They just don't like people to be Americans."

"That's not true," Clifford said. "You know the Chinese word for *American*, but do you know what it really means? The word *ren* means 'people,' *guo* means 'country,' and the word *mei* means 'beautiful.' So *Meiguoren* means 'people of a beautiful country.' It's actually a compliment."

But even so, I still felt as if I were a twisted knot. I was angry at all of them — the bus driver, the convention girls, the market lady. I wanted to yell "I'm American!" but they wouldn't have believed me. Inside, I felt hard and stubborn, like a fist clutching a stolen pearl. I didn't want to learn Chinese, I didn't want to paint bamboo, and I didn't want to be here in Taiwan. Here, people either despised me or acted like I wasn't there, looking through me like a ghost.

Clifford walked with me, pointing out other things and making jokes, so I tried to brush away my hurt feelings. But it was hard. Every time the convention girls' mocking laughter, the market lady's angry voice, or even Audrey Chiang's condescending stare began to fade away, they seemed to come right back to haunt me.

Chapter 21

Temple in Lugang

ghost money

THE NEXT DAY, DAD DECIDED THAT SINCE WE WEREN'T going to go to the cemetery, we should go to Lugang. Aunt Ami and Big Uncle and his friends said it would be a fun place to visit. "It's one of the oldest towns in Taiwan," Dad said. "Also, there's lots of good food there."

old gate in Lugang

The first place we saw when we got there was a famous temple, though it seemed more like a fair than a temple. There was a welcome gate, like the one in Chinatown, but this was much more elaborate and colorful. It was gold and green with detailed carvings of flowers and dragons.

"This gate is very old," Dad said.

"Older than Grandma?" Ki-Ki asked.

"Older than Grandma's grandma," Dad said. "It's one of the oldest things in Taiwan."

Across two of the columns, underneath painted carvings and gold Chinese writing, there was a long screen flashing words in Chinese in electric lights.

"Is that as old as Grandma's grandma, too?" I asked, pointing.

"Well, no," Dad said. "But it's as old as Grandma's granddaughter. It's a gate that crosses all generations!"

Through the gate to the temple, there was a rainbow plastic awning, lines of golden lanterns, and calling vendors with smoking food stalls on either side.

temple in Lugang

129

In the courtyard of the temple, there were tables of food on rough wooden tables. I think the food must have been for ghosts, because no one touched it. There were wax apples and other fruits, but there were also packaged foods, like boxes of tea. There were even packages of Oreo cook-ies! That was a little unex-pected. But I guess there was no reason why ghosts wouldn't like junk food.

package of Oreos

There was also a large stage set up with two peo-ple acting out some sort of play. They wore bright cos-tumes of pink and blue and yellow and strange makeup. Their faces were thickly painted white with brilliant pink cheeks and black eyebrows. Not very natural-looking! In fact, it was the opposite of natural. They looked like aliens. If Mom hadn't told the makeup woman at Lissy's photo shoot to give her a "nat-ural look," I wondered, would Lissy have ended up looking like that? Lissy would have looked awful! But I would've laughed.

opera singer

No one was laughing at these people; instead, there was a big audience watching. The only empty chairs were the ones in the front row, and there were lots of people standing in the back. I wondered why they didn't sit down in the empty seats.

"See that?" Dad pointed. "That's a Chinese opera they are doing."

"Why are they doing opera at a temple?" Lissy asked.

"It's to entertain the ghosts, to show them a good time while they are visiting. And that row?" Dad said, pointing at the empty chairs I had just been wondering about. "No one sits there because those are reserved for the ghosts!"

Everything was a mix of old and new. The temple building was ancient and elegant with intricate carvings and watching lions. It made me feel like I should be quiet and respectful. But the plastic canopy, the brashly colored stage and acting, the loud peddlers, and the junk food made me want to run and yell. Not that I could yell, because there was so much smoke! Everyone seemed to be burning something — incense, ghost money, paper clothes. I watched people buying paper objects from a booth. There were paper dresses and suits wrapped in shirt boxes as if they were from a department store. In other boxes, there were fake teeth, gold watches, perfume, and even computers. I saw packets of ghost money, too, and next to those was a pile of fake American money.

ghost money that looked
like American money

"Those are U.S. bills!" I said, pointing. "Why do they have fake American money?"

"To burn, of course." Dad laughed. "Nowadays, U.S. money is worth more than most other countries' money. People always say American dollars are better, so they think they must be better for the ghosts, too."

We laughed. Through the smoke, I saw Clifford disappearing into the temple and followed him.

"Where are you going?" I asked him.

"I haven't been here in a long time," he said. "The last time was when I was still in high school. I want to see if my green onions are still there."

"What?" I asked as we entered a small room. Clifford went straight to a shrine that had a fancy red and gold case.

In the case was a statue of a bearded man with a gold robe and a round belly. There was a stone table in front of it covered with papers, garlic, radishes, celery, and green onions!

God of Literature
with garlic, radishes,
and celery

"Is he a gardening god or something?" I asked.

"No," Clifford said, and laughed. "He's the God of Literature."

"You gave him onions?" I asked. "Why does he need onions?"

CLIFFORD OFFERS GREEN ONIONS

Like I said, the last time I was here was before I went to college. I visited the summer before I was going to be a senior in high school, the summer before I was going to take the SATs.

It's way too early for you to worry about it, but the SAT is a really important test. If you get a bad score, it can keep you out of the college you want to go to. The better your score, the better school you can get into. I was really nervous about it.

When I told Aunt Ami about the SATs, she told me I should make a prayer to the God of Literature. "Students in Taiwan take many exams," she told me. "And they all make offerings to him for help."

What did I have to lose? I was willing to take any help I could get. Aunt Ami helped me prepare. "What kind of test is it?" she asked. "If you need talent, we'll get a radish. If your test is very detailed and long, you'll need some celery. Or if it is an intelligence test, we'll get green onions."

"What?" I said. "Why do I need those vegetables?"

"They are offerings," Aunt Ami said. "The word for clever in Chinese is 'congming' and the word for onion is 'cong.' See how

they sound alike? So by giving the God of Literature an onion, you are asking for intelligence."

"So the word for radish sounds like talent?" I asked.

"Yes," Aunt Ami said. "And celery sounds like the word diligence — you know, hard-working. Oh, is it a math test? We could bring garlic, too — garlic sounds like the word for count."

I couldn't decide which of them to bring. Really, I felt like I needed all of them. But the SATs are supposed to be some sort of intelligence test, so I decided on the green onions.

When we got here, I watched other students make their offerings. They would place a paper on the table, then their vegetable of choice on top. Then, gravely, they would bow to the God of Literature with a smoking piece of incense. Some wrapped their celery with their papers and tied them, like little presents.

"What are the papers?" I asked.

"Those are their test permits," Aunt Ami said, "so the God of Literature will know which student they're for."

That made sense. There were probably thousands and thousands of students taking tests. But I didn't have a test permit. What was I going to do?

"Just write your name on a piece of paper," Aunt Ami said.

But that didn't seem enough to me. There were probably a lot of Clifford Lins in the world. In fact, there was another Clifford Lin right in my school. How would the God of Literature know which one to help out? I thought hard. Well, how did the gov-

ernment know which Clifford I was? My Social Security number! That was it!

So, on a piece of paper, I wrote my name and Social Security number. I rolled the paper around the onions and tied it with a red string. I placed it on the table and took a piece of incense. As I bowed, I thought, Mr. God of Literature, please help me out on my SATs. I really need a good score. I'm all the way in the United States, so you might have to travel a bit, but you should be able to find my test using my Social Security number. Thanks.

And then I almost started to laugh. But I held it in until we left the temple. It seemed so silly, and I felt a bit foolish. I didn't tell anyone what I had done. I was a little embarrassed.

"Did it work?" I asked. Maybe I should ask the God of Literature to help me paint better than Audrey Chiang. I wondered if she knew about him. If she did, she probably brought a whole wheelbarrow of vegetables every day. "How did you do on your SATs?"

"You know, I did pretty well," Clifford said. "And I even got into the college I wanted to, too. So maybe it did work. That's why I wanted to see the God of Literature again."

With that, Clifford took a piece of incense and bowed. "Thanks, God of Literature," he said. "You're a good guy!"

And we both burst into laughter.

Chapter 22

The **Four Pleasures** of **Life**

dragon fountain

AFTER THAT, I WANDERED THE TEMPLE. IT WAS BIG, WITH different rooms. One room was filled with brilliant gold statues; there was so much bright gold that it hurt my eyes. At home, I had read a story about King Midas, who was granted the wish of turning everything he touched into gold. I imagined that room to be like his home after he touched it.

But most of the temple was filled with the heavy smell of incense and smoke. The ancient, elaborate carvings on the walls and ceiling were the same color as the dark smoke. People were bowing and crowding around a black statue of a round-faced woman, and I knew there was probably a lot to see, but the smoke made me cough at every turn.

So when I saw Ki-Ki at the fountain in the back courtyard, I joined her. There were a lot of kids at the fountain, kneeling on the ledge and leaning against the railing. In the jade-green water, an ancient stone dragon seemed to be climbing out to yell to the sky. The water spurted white against its green moss-covered body and orange-and-white carp swam around it like dancing jewels. The whole thing looked like a painting.

Lissy and Clifford came up next to us. "Too busy in the temple," she said. "Too much smoke and too much noise."

"Yeah, it's different from a church, isn't it?" Clifford said.

That was true. Churches at home were always clean and quiet with people speaking in whispers. Here, it was dirty from smoke and incense, and loud with people talking and kids screaming across the courtyard.

"Churches are more serious," I said.

"I don't know if they are more serious—a lot of people here believe deeply," Clifford said. "But there is definitely more of a sense of humor. Did you see the four little statues on the gate over there?"

We shook our heads.

"They are supposed to represent the best pleasures in life," he said, "which are—yawning, picking your ears, scratching your back, and picking your nose!"

"No!" we all said in unison, giggling. "Gross!"

"It's true!" Clifford said. "I'll show you the sign on the way out."

"Those aren't the best pleasures, though," Lissy said. "What fun is picking your ears or your nose?"

"Well," Clifford asked, "what do you think the best pleasures are, then?"

"Shopping," Lissy said. "Or maybe watching TV."

"Eating candy!" Ki-Ki said.

"No! Eating dumplings!" I said.

the statue for the pleasure of yawning

"We could just say eating," Clifford said. "All right, I choose laughing. That's my greatest pleasure. Pick the last one, Pacy."

I thought hard. Greatest pleasure...what did I like to do the most?

the statue for the pleasure of picking your ears

I wanted to say making art, but I thought about my class and painting next to Audrey Chiang. That wasn't a pleasure at all. I liked writing, too, but it wasn't the writing that gave me the greatest pleasure. I liked it best when people read my writing and liked it. That's what made me happiest.

the statue for the pleasure of picking your nose

the statue for the pleasure of scratching your back

"Reading!" I said.

"Reading?" Lissy said, wrinkling her nose. She was disappointed, probably because she didn't like books so much. "You and books. Boring!"

"Hey, I think reading is a good one!" Clifford said before I could make any remarks about shopping being boring. "I think just being able to read is really one of the greatest pleasures in life, and not just reading books."

"What do you mean?" Ki-Ki asked.

"Well, when I first came to Taiwan, I could barely read anything," Clifford said. "And I remember the first time I went into a store and I could read the signs. I felt so happy. It was truly a great pleasure!"

We laughed. I sort of saw what he meant. In some ways, not being able to read the papers or signs or menus was worse than not being able to speak. All the unreadable words felt like a secret that everyone knew except me.

"You know, the longer I've been here," Clifford said, "the more I realize how hard it must've been for our parents, moving to the United States. It's all the little things, like not being able to read signs or understand directions, that make things so hard."

Mom and Dad had told us about how they had moved to the United States, but I hadn't thought about their not understanding TV commercials, not being able to order food, being ignored because you didn't speak the language — all the things I found hard here in Taiwan. Maybe when Mom

139

and Dad were first in America, everything was just as strange and confusing to them as Taiwan was to me now. It was surprising to think about.

"Good! I'm glad!" Ki-Ki said loudly, shocking us all.

"Glad about what?" Lissy asked.

"That reading is a pleasure," Ki-Ki said. "Because I know how. I can read chapter books all by myself now."

"That is good," Clifford said, laughing. "And think of the even greater pleasures in your future!"

bullet train

EVEN THOUGH IT WAS TWO DAYS LATER, IT SEEMED LIKE almost as soon as we got back from Lugang, we were saying good-bye to Clifford, Lian, Big Uncle, and Aunt Ami and getting on a train back to Taipei. Aunt Ami didn't want us to go. "It's because you'll be traveling into the night," Clifford told us. "She's afraid of ghosts!"

I had laughed then, but as I sat on the train watching the sky get darker and darker, I did feel a tiny bit worried.

"Do they really say if you travel at night, ghosts will come?" I asked.

"Oh, yes," Dad said. "And there are even more superstitions. If you whistle at night, you're inviting ghosts."

"They say the same thing about cutting your fingernails," Mom said. "If you cut them at night, you are inviting ghosts, too."

That just seemed silly! We all laughed at that.

"But we don't really believe in any of those things," Mom said.

"Some people do," I said, thinking of Aunt Ami.

"Yes, that's true," Mom said. "But Grandma and Grandpa always discouraged our family from all that. Some traditions were fine to practice, but they said you also had to use your common sense."

"What do you mean?" Lissy asked.

"Like when my aunt Suying was married," Mom said.

GRANDMA BREAKS TRADITION

When Aunt Suying was to be married, her parents consulted a fortune-teller for a favorable wedding day. This was a custom back then, to ensure a lucky and long marriage, and her parents took this very seriously. The fortune-teller, an old and wrinkled woman, took all the details of the birthdates of both the bride and the groom. Not just the date — the time they were born, too. With that information, she calculated the day and time they should be married.

"September ninth is good," she told them. "But the marriage must take place during the mao period."

Suying's parents were surprised. Each Chinese day was divided into twelve periods, each period two hours long. The mao period was early in the morning, 5 AM to 7 AM! Still, that was

142

Branch	Time
子 zǐ	2300-0100 hrs
丑 chǒu	0100-0300 hrs
寅 Yín	0300-0500 hrs
卯 Mǎo	0500-0700 hrs
辰 Chén	0700-0900 hrs
巳 sì	0900-1100 hrs
午 Wǔ	1100-1300 hrs
未 Wèi	1300-1500 hrs
申 Shēn	1500-1700 hrs
酉 Yǒu	1700-1900 hrs
戌 Xū	1900-2100 hrs
亥 Hài	2100-2300 hrs

day calendar for Chinese fortune-telling

the luckiest time, so they made the preparations accordingly.

The night before the wedding, Suying had a sleepover bridal shower. All her friends from school, cousins, and sisters came. Grandma went, too. It was a fun time with all the girls laughing and talking. They didn't go to bed until very late.

It ended so late that everyone had a hard time waking up in the morning. And they were supposed to wake up early! When Suying finally woke up, it was already time to go.

What a panic it was! Aunt Pinmei was there to do Suying's hair. She was the "good-luck woman." According to tradition, the bride's hair must be arranged by a married woman with many children and a good husband, so that the good luck would be passed on to her. The good-luck woman was supposed to speak auspicious words while she combed the bride's hair and placed on the headdress.

But Suying was already so late that everyone was frantic. Aunt Pinmei could only quickly stammer a couple of lucky phrases as she coiled Suying's hair and stabbed in the bridal comb.

"It's crooked!" Suying wailed as she looked at herself in the mirror. The comb with its red tassels perched awkwardly on her head, with one tassel hung over one ear and the other tassel below her other ear. She reached to fix it.

143

Aunt Suying on her wedding day

"No!" Aunt Pinmei said, pushing her hands away. "You can't redo it! It would be bad luck. You can only do it one time. It's like marriage—once it is done, you have to keep it!"

Suying would have argued, but she was too busy getting pushed out the door to the wedding. She made it just in time, and they were married before the mao period ended. Grandma said no one really remembers the ceremony because they had to do it so fast.

After the ceremony, Suying and her husband were sent to the wedding chamber. Relatives, aunts, and uncles were positioned outside the room—sometimes with teases and jokes, sometimes with food. But there was always someone there, guarding the door, because according to tradition, brides were not supposed to leave the wedding room until the morning after the ceremony.

Now this was fine most of the time, but Suying had been rushed in there at seven in the morning, and there was no bathroom in the bedroom!

By the middle of the afternoon, she, of course, had to use the bathroom. But every time she poked her head out, someone was there, stopping her from leaving the room. Her aunts and mother shook their heads at her. "Hold it," they told her. "It will be bad luck if you leave. You'll have a bad marriage."

Finally, it was Grandma's turn to watch the door. Everyone else had gone downstairs as Suying poked her head out again. "I really need to go!" she whispered urgently. "Pleeaaaase!"

Grandma looked at Suying's begging face. To her, this was not the way a bride should spend her wedding day. A crooked hairstyle, a prisoner in a bedroom — how could any of this ensure a happy marriage? This was just a lot of silliness! At the very least, a woman should be allowed to use the bathroom.

Grandma checked to make sure no one else was around. "Quickly," she said, and motioned Suying out of the room. Suying ran to the bathroom and back without anyone else knowing.

"Thank you!" Suying whispered, and she was so grateful. Grandma was the only one willing to break the tradition and overlook the superstition. Suying was very thankful and remembered it always.

"In fact," Mom said, "she still thanks Grandma for it, even now."

"How was her marriage?" Lissy asked. "Was it still lucky?"

"Yes," Mom said. "She and Uncle Wu have a big house in Fresno now and two sons. One is a doctor, and the other is a computer programmer, and everyone is very happy. So as you can see, all those superstitions aren't really true."

That story made me feel a little better. I also hoped that when I got married, there would be a bathroom in my room.

Chapter 24

BacK in Taipei

the sculpture in front of the
tower that was supposed to
symbolize coins with the holes making
the numbers 101

RETURNING TO TAIPEI ALSO MEANT COMING BACK TO
Chinese painting class. Audrey Chiang hadn't changed at
all. If anything, she was worse. The class had stopped painting bamboo and had moved on to flowers, but I couldn't
even get excited about using my color paints, because I was
too busy trying to get my art talent working. It would show
up only once in a while, and I didn't understand why. The
fortune-teller had said my special skill would be used all my
life. Why did it keep disappearing? It made me hollow and
fragile, like an empty eggshell. Compared with Audrey's pre-
cise, clean flowers, mine looked like pink gum balls melted
into one another. I hated it when Audrey would glance over
with one of her disdainful looks. And she couldn't hide her
satisfaction when the teacher stopped me from painting the
sky blue.

"But my plum blossom branch is outside," I said. "A blue sky will make it look more real."

"Remember," the teacher said, "in Chinese painting, we are painting the idea of how things look, not how they look for real."

His words reminded me of how Dad had said Taichung was more "real Taiwan." And that was still puzzling to me as well. Even after being there, I didn't know what was more real about it.

"I was wrong," Dad said when I asked him later. "Taipei, Taichung—it's all real Taiwan. Because Taiwan is both old and new, modern and traditional. You're right."

I wasn't sure what I was right about. But I guessed that Taipei was the "modern" Dad meant. Because it was only when we got back that I noticed how large and clean the sidewalks were. So far, to me, "modern" meant it was a lot easier to walk around.

But all that was forgotten because Dad was starting to pack his suitcases. He was leaving, going back home tomorrow. That meant thirteen days until we went back home.

"Don't you want to stay for Grandma's birthday party?" Ki-Ki asked him.

"Of course I want to," Dad said. "But I can't. These were the only days I could get off from the hospital. Anyway, there will be so many people at the party, no one will even notice I'm not there."

"But you're going to miss everything!" Ki-Ki said.

"I will be missing some things," Dad said. "But not every-thing. Before I go, we'll go see Taipei 101!"

"What's that?" Lissy asked.

"It's Taiwan's most famous building!" Dad said. "I'm sure you've seen it from a distance. It's the tallest building. In fact, it's the tallest in the world!"

"Second-tallest," Mom said. "There is one in Dubai that is taller."

"Still," Dad said, "it is Taiwan's shin-ing modern icon! We'll all go before I have to go back."

As the taxi drove us there, I did recog-nize it. Taipei 101 had always been in the landscape. It was made of blue-green glass that matched the deepest part of the sky and looked like stacked boxes reaching high above all the other build-ings.

"Is the address 101?" I asked as we got out of the taxi. "Is that why it's called Taipei 101?"

Taipei 101
building

"No," Mom said. "It's because it has 101 floors."

"Why?" Ki-Ki asked.

"It's symbolic," Dad said. "It was built for the new century plus all the new years after. So that is why it's one hundred plus one. One hundred years, one hundred floors, and one symbolic extra for the extra years to come."

I stared up at the building. It was very, very tall! The glass sparkled in the sun, and I got dizzy trying to see the top of the building.

"See that?" Dad said, pointing at what I had thought was just a sculpture of three huge stone circles. "Those are to symbolize ancient Chinese coins. Back then, coins had holes in them. See how the holes make the numbers 101?"

Lissy had also been staring up at the building. "Is that round thing on the side of the building a coin, too?" she asked, squinting.

"Yes," Mom said. "Coins are good-luck symbols."

"Why?" Ki-Ki asked.

"Because they are money!" Mom laughed. "So they mean wealth — which is lucky!"

"Let's go in!" Lissy said. "I don't want to just look at the building all day."

"Okay, okay," Dad said as we went inside. "Should we eat or look first?"

I was going to say eat, but Mom said, "Let's look first. Going up the elevator might upset our stomachs."

We went to the fifth floor and got our tickets. The word OBSERVATORY was above the counter.

"It's in English!" I said, pointing, as we waited in line.

"A lot of things will be in English here," Mom said. "This is a famous tourist place, so things will be in a lot of languages. People from all over come here."

Mom was right. As we crowded onto the big elevator, two people I guessed were Americans got on the elevator after us. They were a couple. The woman's light skin was so blotchy red from sunburn, she was like the colors of strawberries and cream. Her husband was tall and bearded, with sandy hair. They stuck out among everyone else in the elevator, like sunflowers in a daisy patch. Looking at them made me see how we must look in New Hartford. I wondered how they felt.

As the elevator doors closed, a pretty Taiwanese lady in a black uniform began to welcome us. First she spoke in Taiwanese, then Chinese, then Japanese, and then English! A lot of languages really were used here.

"This is one of the fastest elevators in the world," the uniformed lady said in her accented English. "It travels 1,010 meters in one minute. So to take us from the fifth floor to the eighty-ninth floor, it will take thirty-seven seconds."

"That's fast," the American lady said.

"Yeah," her husband said. "Fastest elevator I've ever been in!"

As they spoke to each other, I realized they probably thought that we were Taiwanese or Japanese and couldn't understand them. It gave me a strange feeling. I wanted to say something to tell them we were American, too. But I didn't want them to think I was listening to their conversation, either, so I kept quiet.

The elevator began to move, and the lights dimmed. Above, on the ceiling, twinkled hundreds of tiny lights, arranged just like the night sky. I stared with my mouth open. On the wall, an oval screen lit up with an image of the building and numbers next to it with floor, height, speed, and time on it. The numbers flashed as we passed floors. The elevator was fast! So fast! Tenth floor! Thirty-seventh floor! Two hundred and fifty meters! Three hundred and forty meters! The numbers that told the speed of the elevator went so fast that they blurred, and I couldn't read them. Faster and faster we went. I thought I would feel dizzy or my ears would plug up like they did on the airplane, but neither happened. It was a really modern elevator!

The doors opened, and we emptied out onto a floor that was completely walled in by glass. Past the stalls selling souvenirs and postcards, the world stretched below— buildings, trees, cars, streets, people, all smaller than dollhouse miniatures. I felt as if I were standing on a cloud looking at the earth below. I hadn't realized Taipei was so big. It always looked so small when I saw it on a map. There were so many buildings, but there were also green mountains around everything, too. The mountains layered upon one another in softer and softer colors until they matched the color of the sky and melted away.

I walked aimlessly, looking through the glass at the city below all around. At every corner, there was a plaque with the history of the building and other information. I found Lissy reading one of them. Mom was helping Ki-Ki see through one of the tall standing binocular machines.

"It says this building is shaped to look like bamboo," Lissy said.

"It is?" I said, surprised. I thought about the bamboo I had painted in class. I could see that the segments that joined together to make a stalk of bamboo were kind of like the stacked glass shapes of the building.

"And there are eight sections," Lissy said, "because eight is a lucky number. It sounds like the Chinese word for *prosperity*."

highest
mailboxes in
the world
(I think)

"You don't have to tell me," I said, standing closer to the sign. "I can read, too."

But past the sign, I saw a post office. No, not exactly a post office, but a mailing area. There was a big sign that said MAILBOX AIRMAIL with round mailboxes underneath playfully labeled. One box said FAMILY on a colored striped background, another said FRIEND in blue and white, and the last one said

LOVER on a big red heart. Behind the mailboxes was a counter where people could write their messages on postcards. I watched as the Ameri-

place we could write postcards

can couple from the elevator dropped their postcards into the box that said FAMILY.

"They're the highest mailboxes in the world!" Lissy said. I didn't know if she read that or thought of it herself, but I was excited.

"Let's mail something!" I said, and immediately thought of Melody. It gave me a little shock that I hadn't thought about her in such a long time. It wasn't that I had forgotten about her, exactly, but at home I had been used to her being with me, so I missed her a lot. Here, I wasn't expecting her to be with me, so I didn't feel lonesome. But she was still the person I wanted to send a postcard to the most.

Lissy and I both rushed over to Mom to get her to buy us postage stamps and postcards. Of course, then Ki-Ki wanted to buy them, too, even though she had no one to send post-cards to.

"We can buy this ten-pack of postcards," Mom said, "and you can share."

I didn't like that, because the postcards in the ten-pack were all of the Taipei 101 building at nighttime and with fireworks. And we were in the building during the day. I didn't want Melody to think I had seen the building when there were fireworks. It would have been kind of like lying. And I would've rather picked the special wood postcards that were on display—cards that were made of paper-thin wood with pictures that looked like they had been burned onto it. But when I showed them to Mom, she just looked at the price and wrinkled her nose. "The ten-pack is a much better deal," she said, and I knew that was what we were getting.

We split up the cards (Mom took one for herself so that they would be divided evenly among the three of us) and went to the counter near the mailboxes. I put my postcard to Melody in the FRIENDS mailbox. I chose the card with the

POSTCARD

Dear Melody,
   I'm sending this
to you from the
highest mailbox in
the world (I think)! I
am in Taiwan in the
famous building that's
on the front of the postcard.
It is hot here. I ate raw
fish! And chicken feet (by mistake).
   More later because I'm running out of room. ♡ Pacy

Melody Ling
2328 Palm Ave.
Diamond Bar,
CA
92168

sunset behind the building. That was the most like what I actually saw here in Taiwan. I felt I should send postcards to my friends Becky and Charlotte, too, but I couldn't remember their addresses. I could picture their houses and the streets they lived on, but I had never had to mail anything to them before, so their addresses were just a big blank. Oh well. Mom said the postcards wouldn't get there for two weeks anyway. Maybe I'd just mail them from home and pretend I sent them from Taiwan, though I guess the stamp would give that away.

I looked at the other mailboxes — there was also a mailbox for FAMILY, but Lissy and Ki-Ki and Grandma and Grandpa were here in Taiwan, and I'd never sent anything to any other family before, so it'd seem weird to do it now. The last box had a big red heart on it that said LOVER. I definitely didn't have a card to put in that box, either. The only boy I liked in school was Sam Mercer, and I wasn't going to send him a postcard from Taiwan. Then he would know I liked him!

At the counter, there were also stamps and red ink pads. When I stamped one onto my postcard, it showed a little picture of the building and said TAIPEI 101 at the bottom.

"I'm done," Lissy said. "I'm going to put mine in the mailbox."

"What did you write?" I asked, looking over her shoulder.

"Hey!" Lissy said, hiding her card. "That's private!"

"It's a postcard!" I said. "It can't be that private. Did you write secrets or something?"

"No," Lissy said. "Just the normal things, like 'I'm in Taiwan, having a great time, blah, blah, blah.'"

"Are you having a great time?" I said. "You don't seem like it."

"Sure," she said. "I don't like class, but the rest is okay. Most of the time, the food is good, it's nice to see Grandma and everyone, and it's kind of interesting to see all the different Taiwan stuff."

That was true. "But I don't like how everyone here in Taiwan acts like we're dumb because we don't speak Chinese," I said.

"Yeah," Lissy agreed. "That's no fun. Now that I'm here, I wish I knew Chinese. Maybe I can learn it later and come back. That would make it better."

"Maybe," I said. I wouldn't mind knowing Chinese, but learning it seemed kind of hard. And it was also hard to think about coming back for another trip. This one wasn't even finished yet.

"But it is annoying now," Lissy continued. "Everyone gives us that stupid, shocked look like we just swallowed a cow or something when they find out we don't know Chinese. Then they ignore us."

"Yeah!" I said, nodding hard. I hadn't realized how much Lissy felt like I did. I knew she didn't like class, but knowing she felt invisible sometimes, too, was comforting.

"Not speaking Chinese is probably the worst thing so far,"

Lissy said. "That and class...and the toilets are gross, too. People don't flush their toilet paper; they throw it out in the basket. It's so disgusting."

"Yeah!" I said again. We laughed. I was surprised. Sometimes, when she forgot she was a teenager, Lissy was actually nice to talk to.

"But the rest of it," Lissy said, "is not bad, don't you think?"

Before I could answer, Ki-Ki announced, "I'm done!" She slapped her pen down with a decisive *clack!* and held her postcard in her hands triumphantly, as if it were a prize.

"What did you write, Ki-Ki?" Lissy asked. Ki-Ki, unlike me and Lissy, had liked her class from the start and still did. She didn't worry about whether her paper cuts were good, and she was making lots of friends. "Everyone wants to sit next to me," she had said, "so I can teach them English words."

"Things," she said vaguely but proudly. I couldn't imagine it being that interesting. Ki-Ki marched over to the mailboxes. Slowly but deliberately, she took her postcard and pushed it through the slot of the box that said LOVER! Lissy and I stared open-mouthed.

"Ki-Ki has a boyfriend!" Lissy said as Ki-Ki walked back toward us. "Ki-Ki, who's your boyfriend?"

"No one!" Ki-Ki said, scowling at our giggles. "I don't have a boyfriend!"

"Well, then who did you mail your postcard to?" I asked.

"Who else would you mail a postcard to from the LOVER box?"

"I mailed it to myself," Ki-Ki said, sticking her chin up. "I didn't have anyone to send a postcard to except myself. And I love myself, so I put my postcard in there."

Lissy and I burst out into loud laughter, and Ki-Ki joined in. So silly! And I realized that maybe Lissy was right. Even though I didn't love being in Taiwan as much as Ki-Ki loved herself, maybe it wasn't so bad after all.

Chapter 25

Dumplings at Taipei 101

McDonald's rice burger

"THE FIRST FIVE FLOORS OF THIS BUILDING ARE A MALL," Dad said, "and in the basement is the food court."

"Let's go there!" I said. "I'm hungry!"

Back in New Hartford, at the Sangertown Square Mall, there was a food court with about a dozen fast-food restaurants. It was kind of dark, with brown plastic tables and chairs and fake plants and flower arrangements that looked kind of dusty. I was expecting the food court here, especially since Dad said it was in the basement, to look the same.

But it didn't at all. The food court was shiny and white, the floor so clean that it sparkled. And there was so much food! There was a bakery with cakes of bread wrapped in plastic and frosted pink donuts that looked like baby rattles. There were restaurants with glass cases displaying plates of shiny plastic food and others that had huge mountains of fried rice and noodles on the counters. One restaurant had pale chickens hanging in its case, their heads still on. I had seen that in Chinatown but never in a mall!

And the best thing was that a lot of places had Chinese and English. I could read almost everything! Premier Beef Noodle had noodles with clear soup and soy soup. Sergeant Chicken Rice had a chicken rice bowl and chicken liver (yuck!).

That's also when I noticed that there were all kinds of foods at the food court. There was a French pastry place and an Indian place. There was an Italian place called Benito

the Italian fast-food restaurant at the food court

and a Japanese restaurant called Karen. There were so many places, I didn't know what to choose.

Until Ki-Ki shouted, "Look! McDonald's!"

Lissy and I rushed over to where Ki-Ki was pointing. There really was a McDonald's. There was the big, glowing yellow M, just like the McDonald's we had at home. Suddenly, I missed New Hartford. I missed our white house with green shutters, the big green lawn and trees. I missed talking to Melody on the phone, my friends in my class, the orange brick library, and even my box-shaped school. Seeing McDonald's here was like seeing something from home. It made me excited, like finding a lost shoe.

"Let's eat there!" I said.

"Really?" Dad said. "You want McDonald's?"

"*Yes!*" Lissy, Ki-Ki, and I said in unison.

"Okay." Dad shrugged. "*Mai Dang Lao.*"

"*Mai Dang Lao?*" I asked. "Is that what they call McDonald's here?"

"Yes." Dad nodded and laughed. "When there are Western words that there are no Chinese words for, they just put together Chinese words that sound like English."

"Really?" I said. "What else?"

"Um..." Dad thought hard. "Like hamburger. We pronounce it 'hanbao'!"

"And chocolate," Mom said, "is pronounced like 'chokoli.'"

We laughed. It was funny how it sounded the same but different. I wished all Chinese words were like that. It would've been a lot easier for me to learn Chinese that way.

Well, not only was McDonald's not called exactly the same thing in Taiwan, but it also didn't look exactly the same, either. This McDonald's was a lot cleaner and brighter, with white floors and walls and wood tables. It wasn't anything like the plastic red and yellow tables we had in New Hartford.

And the food was different, too. As we stood in line and looked at the glowing menus overhead, I was confused. Only some words were in English, like EXTRA VALUE MEAL, but the rest were in Chinese. There were photos of food, but some of them were pictures I had never seen in a McDonald's before. On a banner, there was a photo of round fried balls next to a bowl of corn soup. Corn soup? At McDonald's? Also, in some of the photos, there were fried chicken and weird-looking hamburgers with buns that looked like thick, sesame-sprinkled rice crackers.

"What are those?" I asked, pointing.

Mom looked at the photos. "Rice burgers," she said. "Do you want one?"

I shook my head. "I want chicken nuggets," I said.

Ki-Ki and I got the chicken nuggets, and Lissy got fried chicken. Mom ordered for us. We had gotten used to Mom and Dad doing all the ordering and talking, but I never really got used to the questioning looks the clerks gave us when Mom spoke to us in English.

"It comes with a side order," Mom said, "of french fries or corn. Which do you want?"

"Corn?" I asked, and I noticed another customer's order to our side. There was a small cup of corn kernels on his tray. Weird! "French fries!" I said. Lissy and Ki-Ki ordered the same. Mom and Dad got the rice burgers and a bowl of corn soup each.

Cup of corn

The rice burger came in a green cardboard container, kind of the same as how a large order of fries was packaged back home, except with a lid. It was strange to see the yellow M logo with Chinese writing. Dad lifted the lid of his container, took out his rice burger, and unwrapped it from the wax paper so we could see it. The bun wasn't a rice cake or a rice cracker, like I had thought it'd be. It was rice tightly packed and toasted to make a bun shape. Instead of a meat patty and pickles, there was pork with slices of lettuce.

"Want to try?" Dad said, offering it to us.

I hesitated, but Lissy took a big bite. She chewed slowly. "Hmm," she said.

"Is it good?" I asked.

"It's not bad," she said slowly. "But it's not a hamburger."

Well, I had to try it then. I took a bite, and the rice bun crumbled and began to fall apart. But it was moist and soft, and the pork was covered with a sweet sauce. It tasted like a Chinese pork dish Mom made at home, but it was shaped like a hamburger.

"I think you are supposed to eat it with the paper wrapper around it," Mom said, "so that the rice doesn't make such a mess."

But I had had enough of bizarre McDonald's food. I wanted the real stuff. I dipped my chicken nuggets in honey and chewed away. *Ahh! Just like home.*

"What's for dessert?" I asked when we finished.

"Let's look around," Dad said as he threw out our tray. "You know, this is the first meal we've had that Pacy hasn't eaten dumplings."

That wasn't exactly true, but it was the first time we had eaten that I hadn't thought about dumplings. I frowned. I felt like I was losing some kind of bet.

Dad stopped us in front of a display case of hundreds of pretty round balls dusted with sugar like little snowballs. Some were pale pink, others a soft gray-green, and there were even light yellow ones, the color of buttercups.

"Are they chocolate?" Lissy asked. "Chocolate truffles?"

"No," Dad said. "*Mochi.* We'll get some of these. You should try it."

I took one of the pale pink ones, the same color as the peonies Mom grew at home. The

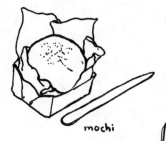

mochi

fine sugar dust sprinkled down my shirt as I bit into it. The *mochi* had a smooth skin, soft and chewy. A strawberry-flavored, creamy filling oozed into my mouth, with a smell even sweeter than the taste. The whole thing blended together and seemed to melt in my mouth. It was delicious.

"Like it?" Dad asked us.

We nodded and reached for more.

"You know what *mochi* really is?" I asked.

"What?" Dad said.

"It's a dessert dumpling!" I said.

"Oh, is it?" Dad said, laughing. "Does this mean you have eaten dumplings every day since you've been in Taiwan?"

"Almost!" I said, and grinned.

the teacher's fancy
chops

"THIS IS OUR LAST WEEK OF CLASS," THE TEACHER SAID
to us the next morning. "So in the next few days, you must
choose which painting you want to show in our exhibit."

Exhibit! I remembered he had said something about that
on the first day of class, but I hadn't remembered it until now.
Audrey Chiang waved her hand in the air as if it were a flag.

"Is there going to be a prize at the exhibit?" she asked.
"For the best painting?"

"Yes," the teacher said, and smiled. "The teachers usually
honor the painting they like best with a ribbon."

"Only one?" Audrey asked. "Only for the best?"

"Well, one for each class. You know there are other classes
here, right? For Chinese writing and other things," he said,
and then repeated himself as he often did. "So one in this
class."

Audrey sat up straight, as if she had already won. She wasn't really doing anything — yet I still wanted to slap her.

"But before anyone can be awarded a ribbon, you must learn how to make a painting," he said.

That was confusing. Hadn't we been making paintings all this time?

"Up to now, I have been just teaching you elements," he said, as if reading my mind. "Bamboo, flowers, birds — it is how you put them together that makes a painting. Most students spend years just painting bamboo, but this course is just to give you a taste of how to paint. So today, I will show you how to make a painting, and then you can try your own."

I still didn't really understand all that he was saying, a little bit because of his accent and his stuttering. He motioned for all of us to stand around him like we did the first day. As he lay a piece of snow-white rice paper down on the table in front of him, using his carved paperweights to hold it down, I found myself standing next to Audrey Chiang. I tried not to look at her. The teacher fingered his bamboo paintbrushes

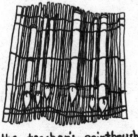

the teacher's paintbrushes

lovingly, finally choosing one and swirling it in the water and ink. And then, just like he did the first day of class, he made just a few strokes, and a bamboo stalk grew on the paper. He added more leaves and crimson flowers.

"For painting," he said, "it is about composition and balance. You don't want everything to be busy. You need an area of focus, but also the other areas to balance it."

His hands lingered over his brushes, as if deciding. Then his hand swooped down, quickly seizing one. His fingers reminded me of chopsticks picking the best pieces of meat from a dish. Then he seized another brush and circled it in the pink paint he had just used to paint plum blossoms, and he painted a bird flying on the bare side of the page.

After struggling to paint a bamboo leaf right, I felt awed. Each stroke was strong and certain and his hands quick and controlled, blotting and brushing in a graceful dance. His eyes darkened in concentration, and every one of us watched, mesmerized. He took his name chop and pressed a red mark into the painting.

the teacher's painting

"Everything in the painting must be balanced," he said. "Even your mark has to be placed carefully; it's part of the painting. The red color has to be balanced — it can't be too close or too far from elements. Never put your mark on top of a bird or in the middle of your bamboo."

"What does the stamp say?" Eva, the girl with the long hair, asked.

"Li Mengshan," the teacher said. "My name!"

I was glad I finally learned his name. It was kind of funny that it was only today, during this last week of class, that I learned what it was. But in a strange way, it was kind of fitting, too. Because after watching him paint, I felt like I was meeting him for the first time. I remembered on that first day, I just supposed he wasn't a good artist, because he couldn't speak well. He spoke English so hesitantly, bumbling and stumbling over words, I had thought that was the kind of person he was. And he wasn't. I realized that was probably how people saw me here because I couldn't speak Chinese. They thought because I couldn't speak the language, I didn't have anything important to say.

"I don't have a name chop," Eva said.

"It's okay," the teacher said. "I have some you can use."

"But then our paintings will have *your* name on it!" Audrey sputtered.

"No, you won't use this chop, the one with my name," the teacher said. "I have others."

And he reached over and untied a small roll of cloth. Inside lay three more chops. The figures on top were beautiful, bigger, and more intricately carved than my tiger. One chop was made out of red stone with gray flecks in it, and the top had a carving of two fish swimming on a wave of water. Another was a creamy ivory color with a bamboo carving, and the one with the lotus flower was gray with muted orange and brown shining through.

"These are my chops for different moods," he said. "Sometimes I add another mark with my name to add to the mood of the painting. I have some at home I will bring for you to choose from. You can borrow them for your painting if you don't have your own. In the future, maybe you can add your own to it."

"What do these say?" I asked. These must be chops like the one Dad's friend had that said "never too tired for knowledge." It reminded me that we hadn't gotten ours carved yet. I'd have to remind Mom.

"This one," the teacher said, stroking the red stone seal with the carved fish, "says 'this moment will last in my memory.' The gray one says 'spring opens the heart to happiness,' and the bamboo says 'fulfilling wish.' The ones you can borrow, which I will bring, will be more simple, better for you. "

"What will those, the ones we can use, say?" a square-headed boy asked—for some reason I thought his name was Alex, but I wasn't sure.

" 'Joy,' 'love,' 'harmony,' " he said, "that kind of thing. Simple, but it will still look very nice. But when you choose, make sure it matches the mood of your painting. Every detail in your painting is important."

We all went back to our desks. I guessed the simple chops would be okay. Lots of people had nodded when Eva said she didn't have a chop, so most of the class was probably going to use the teacher's chops. But I'd rather have my own. I wondered if I could get mine carved in time for the exhibit. But what would I have carved? It was driving me crazy that I couldn't decide.

Or maybe it was Audrey Chiang who was driving me crazy. I'm sure she would get something like "forever the best" carved on her name chop with plans to decorate it with the winning class ribbon. As she took out her paper, I watched her as she carefully looked around the room at each of the students. There were lots of good painters in our class, but there was no one who I could say was the best. Eva painted bamboo really well and that boy Rex could paint nice flying birds. And I was pretty good, too.

But I could almost see Audrey calculating how to be the best. I was calculating, too. How was I going to beat her? I was not going to let Audrey Chiang win the ribbon in our class. I had a special art talent, and it was not going to let her win. At least, I hoped not.

Chapter 27

Lissy's Photos

Lissy's photo

DAYS WERE MELTING AWAY. DAD HAD LEFT, AND NOW we had only ten days left in Taiwan. Today we were going to the photography studio so Lissy could choose her photos for the album, and tomorrow I had to choose which painting I wanted for the exhibit. Mom had said I had to use the teacher's chop because she didn't have time to get our chops carved. "Later," she'd promised. "I'll get your chops carved later."

Maybe there wasn't any time because everyone was planning for Grandma's birthday party. Aunt Bea had already chosen the restaurant for the party, and Auntie Jin had sent out the invitations before we even arrived in Taiwan. And Uncle Flower, Shogun, Julian, and their father had been and were still practicing "a secret!" Uncle Flower had said.

"What has Grandpa done for the party?" I asked.

"He's too busy working to do anything for the party," Auntie Jin said, laughing. "He's paying for it!"

Mom felt bad that everyone else had done so much work for the party already, so she said she would order the cakes. "We can stop by the bakery on the way back from the photo studio," she said.

Lissy was eager to see her photos. She tried to hide it, but I could tell by the way she tapped her foot on the subway. I was curious, too.

We were kind of taken aback when the woman and the photographer pushed Lissy in front of a computer. But we quickly figured out what was going on. Lissy was supposed to click a little box on the screen if that was a photo she wanted in her album. We all peered at the monitor.

looking at Lissy's photos

"Who's that?" Ki-Ki asked.

"Me!" Lissy said, giving Ki-Ki a don't-be-dumb look.

"No, it's not!" Ki-Ki said. "They mixed your photos up with someone else's. We've got the wrong set."

"No, we don't," Lissy said, sighing in annoyance. "They're my pictures."

I didn't blame Ki-Ki for thinking they weren't Lissy's photos. The girl onscreen had luminous eyes and glowing skin

174

that looked as soft as a freshly laundered bedsheet. Her hair was glossy and smooth like black embroidery floss, and her pink lips formed a delicate doll smile. The girl in the photo was glowing and plastic-looking, like an actress or a movie star. She did not look like Lissy.

And even when we knew it was Lissy, it was still hard to believe. When I looked closely, I could see a small resemblance — the nose, the teeth, the way she held the fan. But it felt like we were looking at a stranger.

"I think they made you taller on the computer," I told her. I couldn't exactly tell what they did, but she sure looked different. "Or something."

Lissy didn't seem to be bothered. She swung her legs as she clicked and scrolled and asked us over and over again which picture we liked better.

"This one with the umbrella?" she'd ask us. "Or the close-up in the rainbow room?"

"I like them both the same," I said. Which was true, because I didn't like either of them.

"Okay, both, then," Lissy said happily. "Mom, there's a little box I can click if I want a poster made. Can I get a poster made?"

A poster! I didn't know if I wanted to see a big-size version of these photos, but Mom said, "Okay, but only one."

I shrugged.

Soon, Ki-Ki and I got bored of watching Lissy go through

her pictures. We left her and Mom at the computer and sat in the waiting area, flipping through magazines. They were all in Chinese, so I couldn't understand them.

Taiwanese fashion magazines

"Look," Ki-Ki said, stopping at a page. "This is the same dress Lissy is wearing in her photos."

It wasn't exactly the same dress, but it was close. But what was weird was how much the model in the magazine looked like Lissy did in her photos. I looked at Lissy at the computer, squinting into the screen with her hair tangled at the ends and her dirty feet in flip-flops. There was no way she looked like a movie star or a model in real life. But if I didn't know her, her photos might have made me think so. If they could make Lissy look like a hairspray model, they could make anyone look like one. I started to flip through the pages of the magazine again and realized—they were all fake! All these fashion models were probably photographed like Lissy, lots of makeup, fake eyes, and lighting and computer changes. It was all a big lie.

I went back over to Lissy. She was almost done.

"You know you don't really look like those photos," I said to her.

"I know," Lissy said. "But it's fun. Like a story or a movie. You don't have to be mean about it."

"No," I said. "I meant you don't look like those photos, and it's good. I think you look a lot better in real life."

"Oh," Lissy said. She didn't say anything else, but a little pleased smile curved on her lips. I'd never really said nice things to Lissy before, but for some reason I felt like this was important. Because it was true. I did think she looked better in real life. She didn't look like someone fake. In real life, she looked like Lissy — someone who was sometimes nice, sometimes mean, but always my sister. Just being herself was much better looking than one of those models pretending in the magazine.

But that meant Lissy kind of was a beautiful thought, then, I realized in surprise. Her Chinese name was right about her. I would never have believed it.

Chapter 28

The Bakery

pineapple
cake

AFTER THE PHOTO STUDIO, WE WENT TO THE BAKERY
so Mom could order the cakes for Grandma's birthday party.
As soon as we entered, a warm, buttery smell filled our
noses. We kept taking deep breaths with our eyes closed,
trying to eat the smell.

But maybe we didn't need to try to eat the smell, because
it looked like there were free samples all over the bakery for
us to taste. There were rows of trays full of all kinds of cakes
and breads and cookies. A lot of things I had never seen before, but everything looked good. Crowded together were
round yellow buns with sandy sugar tops, sunshine-colored
egg tarts like the ones we had eaten at dim sum, and even
bread in the shape of pig heads!

One row was filled with small rectangle cakes — the shape
of toy wooden blocks. Each one was wrapped in plastic and

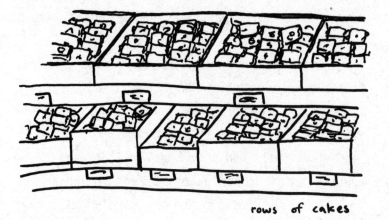

rows of cakes

was a golden, toasted color. I thought they were all exactly the same until I noticed that the sample plates in front of them showed different colored fillings. Mom's eyes lit up when she saw them.

"Pineapple cakes!" she said. "I love these!"

"Are they all pineapple?" I asked.

Mom looked down the aisle. "They make them in many different flavors now," she said. She went to the stack of empty boxes at the side and handed one to each of us. "You can each fill a box with them to bring home."

That was exciting. Lissy, Ki-Ki, and I rushed over to try the samples. But as Lissy reached for a chunk of cake with a nut-colored filling, I suddenly got worried.

pineapple cakes in a box

"They are samples, right?" I said,

179

tugging at her arm. "They aren't food left out for ghosts, are they?"

Lissy's arm froze with her hand hovering over the plate, and we looked at each other. But then a teenage boy passed us, casually took one of the cake pieces, and popped it into his mouth. We grinned. They were samples!

Lissy, Ki-Ki, and I tried every single one. There were cherry, walnut, pineapple, lychee, and egg. The egg-flavored one was kind of peculiar. There were also a couple of cakes that we couldn't tell what the flavors were. There was one with a darkish purple filling and another with an orange filling that didn't taste like orange at all. We agreed that the pineapple ones were the best, with their thin, buttery crust and sweet, firm pineapple filling. I guess that's why they were the original ones.

We could put fourteen cakes in each box, so filling it was a hard decision for me. Lissy put every flavor in her box, even the weird egg one. Ki-Ki just put in all pineapple. I decided to put in mostly pineapple but a couple of the cherry- and walnut-flavored ones, too.

It took us so long to choose our cakes that Mom was waiting for us by the time we had finished. She had talked to the woman at the counter for a while, ordering cakes for the party.

"Did you get pineapple cakes for Grandma's party, too?" Lissy asked as we left. The big bakery bag that held our cakes knocked against her knees.

"No," Mom said. "I ordered special cakes for the party.

Peach buns — remember, like the ones we had with soup dumplings? And turtle cakes."

"Turtle cakes? Not made of turtles, right?" I asked. I didn't think so, but I had to make sure.

"No, it's just a cake that looks like a turtle shell," Mom said. "Turtles mean longevity, too, just like the peaches. It's because turtles are known for living such a long time."

We rode the subway home. It was crowded but not as busy as the first time we rode it. This time Mom let us each scan in our subway token as we went in. The tokens were round, purple, plastic discs that reminded me of toy money. When we got off the subway, we were supposed to drop them into a machine.

The subway car came, and Lissy and I squeezed onto a seat with the bakery bag in our laps. Mom held Ki-Ki's hand with one hand and a silver pole with the other, her bag on her shoulder. Crowds of people pressed into one another, and I watched a

Subway tokens

group of girls giggling and a man trying to read a book as the train swayed. I was getting used to not knowing what people were saying. But not being able to understand Chinese meant that all I did was look at things. And eat — I did that, too.

I remembered the samples I had eaten at the bakery and how I had wondered if they had been for hungry ghosts. I

181

knew they hadn't been, but a small part of me still worried. What if I had eaten food meant for a hungry ghost?

As I sat silently with all the passengers casually ignoring me, I realized that I was like a ghost myself. Everything here—the crowds of people who tried to walk through me, the signs I couldn't read, the words I couldn't say, and even the art I couldn't paint—made me feel like I was invisible. Sometimes I felt like I was disappearing. Just like a ghost.

man pretending to read on subway

The subway lurched, and the doors opened. Mom and Ki-Ki pushed against me as people rushed out. As the man with the book staggered past us, I saw his thin hand reach into Mom's bag! Faster than my mouth could open, a blue change purse from Mom's bag vanished behind his book.

"Mom!" I said, pointing. Lissy saw it, too. "Mom! Mom! Your purse!"

But it was too late. The crowd of people had already thrust him out of the subway, and he was gone.

"He stole something from your bag!" Lissy said, her words running into each other.

Mom's eyes and mouth opened, each making round circles of panic. She quickly opened her bag and started to look through it.

"It was a little blue purse," I said, "in the front pocket."

"My blue purse?" Mom said, and she was still for a moment. Then she started to laugh.

"What's so funny?" we all asked. It didn't seem funny to us at all. Mom had just been robbed!

"That purse had tissues in it!" she said, laughing harder. "Tissues for the bathroom! He stole tissues!"

We all started to laugh then. We laughed so hard that everyone in the subway car looked at us. But we couldn't help it; it was so funny! I wondered what the thief would do when he opened Mom's change purse and just found tissues.

Mom's change purse with tissues in it

The subway car started moving again, and Mom and Ki-Ki tilted forward. When they swayed back, Mom had stopped laughing.

"I always thought they only pickpocketed tourists," Mom said, more to herself than to us. "I guess they can tell that I am not from here anymore."

Mom's face looked kind of sad. I hadn't thought about Mom not being from Taiwan anymore. It was probably weird coming back to Taiwan, the place that used to be her home but wasn't anymore. She was really from America now, just like us. And we were all just like visiting ghosts.

the teacher's chops that we
could use

IT WAS FRIDAY. WE HAD NINE DAYS LEFT IN TAIWAN. IT
was the last day of painting class and the day I had to choose
which painting I wanted in the exhibit. The actual exhibit
wasn't until next week, but we had to hand them in so they
could be mounted.

"Does it have to be mounted?" Rex, the boy who sat next
to Eva, asked.

"Yes," the teacher said, almost astonished that someone
would ask that. "It's very important. Do you see how when
your paint dries, your paper is wrinkled?"

We nodded. I had noticed that. It was a pain. I was always
trying to smooth out my finished pictures.

"When we glue it onto silk, when we mount it in our special way," he said, "the painting becomes flat again and the

silk makes a border. A painting is not considered finished unless there is a border around it."

"Our paintings will be mounted on silk?" I asked. That sounded really fancy!

"Yes," the teacher said again. "Mounting a painting is important. The Chinese word for the mounting silk is *ming zhi* — that means 'life paper.' Mounting your painting brings it to life. That is how a painting is finished."

I was used to the way the teacher spoke now. I didn't mind so much that he repeated himself or didn't really answer the questions we asked. Ever since he had shown us how to make a painting, I respected him a lot. He was a real artist.

I was an artist, too, at least sometimes, when my talent decided to work. But even then, I wasn't as good as he was. So far I had a couple of paintings that I thought were okay, but I kept hoping I'd paint an even better one. I wondered which one of her paintings Audrey was going to choose. She had one with red flowers growing out of old, weathered branches that looked almost like the teacher had done it. I didn't paint flowers as well, I think, because I missed those classes when we went to Taichung.

But I could paint nice birds. I mixed up some carmine-red paint with some white and it made a brilliant pink. It was the same color as those awful pink dresses Mom had made us wear on the plane to Taiwan. I remembered how I had imagined Lissy, Ki-Ki, and I had been bright pink birds and how grumpy I was that we had to come. It seemed such a long time ago. And we would be flying back home soon.

I started to paint three pink birds. One for me, one for Lissy, and one for Ki-Ki. Not bad, but the birds were just floating in the air. They'd be better on a branch or something. Oops, I should have painted a branch first. I took out another sheet of paper. I sighed. It was annoying that I couldn't erase or cover my marks.

I painted an arching bamboo. Was there enough room for the birds? Well, Ki-Ki was small. I felt like I was squeezing both Ki-Ki the bird and my art talent at the same time. C'mon! There! Three birds on a bamboo. A warm, happy feeling filled me, like I had swallowed a bowl of delicious soup.

I leaned back to get a better look at my painting. Yes, this was my best one. I was sure of it. My art talent had been stubborn, but it had appeared this time. I looked over at Audrey, who was looking at my painting fiercely, as if I had written insults on it. Ha! That meant it was good.

I walked up to the teacher's desk. He had brought in the chops for the class to use. They were all simple, without any elaborate carvings, but the smooth stone felt nice in my hand. The teacher knew most of us couldn't read Chinese, so he placed each chop on a piece of paper with the meaning in English written on it. There were a lot of chops, maybe a dozen to choose from. He probably wanted to make sure there were enough choices to match our paintings. Some were the ones he had mentioned earlier — "love," "harmony," "happiness," and "spring." There were also some that I thought were kind of odd for paintings, like "forever," "mercy," and "profundity." I didn't even know what *profundity* meant. I'd have to look it up in the dictionary when I got home.

So which chop matched the mood of my painting? Since the three birds were supposed to be me, Lissy, and Ki-Ki, I wasn't sure which chop to pick. "Harmony" or "peace" wouldn't be true — we always fought about things. "Spring"? Was it spring in my painting? I hadn't really thought about it. The birds were on a bamboo, so it could be any time of year. The teacher had said painting a bamboo meant to wish something. Hmm, what were we wishing for? Not love. That would look stupid.

But I had to decide fast. Class was ending, and the teacher was calling on everyone to give him their paintings. Everyone was frantically sorting through their papers, and there was a mad rush as people clamored around the table to get one of the chops to stamp their paintings. *Which one?* I thought. I grabbed the chop on the paper marked "happiness." I wasn't sure if that was exactly right, but it kind of fit. Lissy, Ki-Ki, and I always wished to be happy, right?

I brought the chop and the red ink over to my desk and quickly but carefully stamped my painting. I made sure to leave plenty of room below the stamp to put my own name chop, whenever we got those.

my painting

Audrey's painting

Maybe that's what the three birds were wishing for, for their name chops to be carved!

I lined up behind Audrey to give the teacher my painting. Over her shoulder, I saw she had chosen the red flower painting. It was really good. Was it better than mine? I looked at my birds. I couldn't really tell. I guess we'd find out at the exhibit.

Chapter 30

The Night Market

woman at night market
making cakes that looked
like hockey pucks

THAT NIGHT UNCLE SHIN ARRIVED. HE HAD COME ALL
the way from Philadelphia to Taiwan for Grandma's party,
and everyone was happy to see him. When he laughed,
everyone else laughed, too. And he laughed a lot. Uncle
Shin was always jolly. Mom said he was a playboy, which I
thought was true because he always likes to play and have
fun. And instead of eating at a restaurant for dinner, Uncle
Shin wanted to go to the night market.

"What's that?" Lissy asked.

"You haven't taken them to the night market!" He looked
at Mom and shook his head. "It's what Taipei is famous
for — the night markets."

"But what is it?" I asked. "Is it just a market at night?"

"Yes," Uncle Shin said, "but not just shopping, like
a flea market. There's lots of food! My favorite food is

always at the night market. It's a lot of fun. You have to see it!"

"Well, they'll see it now." Mom laughed. Aunt Bea called her home to get our cousins Julian and Shogun to meet us there, and we all rushed to leave.

Outside, the sky was the color of ink. When Julian, Shogun, and their father met us, the streetlights shone down and I stared at my long shadow in front of me. Taxis streaked by, their headlights looking like staring eyes in the dark. I remembered how Aunt Ami didn't want us traveling at night during Ghost Month and looked quickly at everyone else. No one seemed worried. In fact, everyone was quite cheerful.

"This way!" Uncle Flower said, leading us down the street. We all followed Uncle Flower like we were in a parade. The noises of the street got louder and louder, and more and more people began to pack around us. A strong, hot smell filled the air, a mix of frying oil and smoke. Glowing signs lit the streets as bright as the sun, making it easy to see the peddlers crowded with their stands of frying foods. It was like a carnival or a fair. It reminded me of being at the temple in Lugang, except it was at night, busier, and, as I soon found out, much bigger.

"Is this the night market?" I asked Uncle Shin. I had to say it loud so he could hear me over all the sounds and clattering of the crowd.

"It's the beginning of it!" he said to me. "There's a lot more!"

I followed him deeper into the masses of people. It felt like everyone in Taiwan was at the night market, too. Everyone was coming and going, pushing and crowding. It was hard to keep my eyes on Uncle Shin when there were so many things to look at. One peddler had piles and piles of meat on sticks laid out on trays in front of a grill. At another stand, a woman was frying six big omelets on a round stove that looked like a metal barrel. Another stand had a steaming hot metal form with circles molded in it, like a line of cups. As the peddler poured in batter, round cakes—the shape of hockey pucks—baked golden brown. I was starting to get hungry.

the night market

"Can we eat?" I yelled to the back of Uncle Shin's shoulder. He nodded and pointed to a cart nearby. When we got there, I saw there was a long line.

"We'll start with this!" he said.

"What is it?" Lissy asked. She, Mom, and Ki-Ki had been right behind me the whole time.

"Chicken cutlets!" Uncle Shin said. "One of the famous foods of the night market. I'll take you to all the famous foods tonight, okay?"

Chicken cutlet

As we waited in line, Ki-Ki tugged on my arm. "Look!" she said.

At the cart next to us, there were fat hot dogs on a stick. But not any hot dogs. These were baked in bread that looked like waffled cones. Some sticks had a wavy line of something that imitated ketchup or mustard on it, but I think it was really frosting. A couple of them had candied eyes on them, and one even had a bow tie!

"Waffle dogs!" I said. "They should make one that looks like a dog!"

We looked at the rows of waffle dogs waiting for buyers. There was one made to look like a baby, with a pink bow,

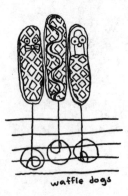
waffle dogs

but no dogs. We were a little disappointed.

Uncle Shin handed each of us a huge chicken cutlet wrapped in paper. It was flat and round and so big that it had to be folded in half for our hands to hold it. It was like a super-extra-large piece of fried dough at a carnival, except it was meat. I didn't think I could finish all of mine, but it was so good! The meat was tender and juicy, and the fried batter was salty and crispy. It was like the best chicken nugget I could imagine — as well as the largest.

We were just taking our second and third bites in the chicken cutlets when Aunt Bea, Shogun, and Julian came up to us. Shogun and Julian were sharing something that looked like a sauce-covered baseball from a carton.

"Everyone else is down there," Aunt Bea said. "They wanted *chou doufu*."

"*Chou doufu!*" Uncle Shin said. "We'll get that next. That's famous, too."

We pushed our way down the street. This was the most crowded place I had ever been. It was busier than the subway, the train station, and the temple in Lugang. The heavy smoke smell of grilled foods and charcoal hung like a fog, and the mixture of all the people talking, bells from nearby games, and music blaring from stores was just a loud, confusing noise. There was a pink booth filled with hanging toys and a row of small, desk-sized pinball machines actually made with real pins and had marbles for balls. One woman laid out clothes on a large cloth in the middle of the road, and we had to squeeze on either side of her display. We even passed a booth selling wigs!

But mostly the night market was full of food. So much!

Little golden cakes in the shape of cute pigs and ducks. Colorful fruits looking like a rainbow on ice. Shiny, egg-shaped sausages. Some things were just weird, like little tomatoes skewered on a stick with a candy coating on them. It was like candy apples—but tomatoes! We had no idea what other things were. "What's that?" we kept asking and pointing. "What's that?"

"Quail eggs," Mom said about some small batter-fried balls with a brown sauce.

"Pig's blood cake," Aunt Bea said about dark, almost black mounds on a silver tray.

"Duck tongues," Uncle Shin said about some deep-fried things that looked like insects. "Want to try some?"

We shook our heads hard, and I started to think maybe we should stop asking. But Lissy pointed at a sign with a drawing of a frog on it, and among all the Chinese writing, there were three English words written exactly like this: WOW FRog egGs.

"Frog eggs!" Lissy said. "Is that a mistake? Did they mean frog legs?"

Either way, I hoped we wouldn't eat there.

Mom looked at the sign and laughed. "No," she said. "They really mean frog eggs. But it's not what you think."

"It's a drink," Uncle Shin said. "Let's get some."

We followed, cautiously, as Uncle Shin bounded over. At the stall a woman was wearing a white apron with the same

194

frog on it as the one on the sign. It didn't say "WOW FRog egGs" on her shirt, though. She was stirring a big silver bowl full of tea-colored water and what looked like clear Jell-O. Behind the bowl were two deep vats we couldn't see inside of.

frog-eggs drink stand

Uncle Shin nodded, ordered, and then passed us each a plastic cup with a straw as wide as my thumb sticking out of it like a flagpole. The cups were full of golden-colored water and ice, but at the bottom, floating around like tadpoles without tails, were round balls.

"What are those?" I asked. "Are those the frog eggs?"

"Those are tapioca," Mom said. "They just call it frog eggs because they think that's how the tapioca looks."

195

I looked again at my cup. They really did look like what I imagined frog eggs would look like. I took a sip. Kind of lemon-tasting but not lemonade. It was cool and sweet. A tapioca pearl rose up the straw and into my mouth. It was smooth and slippery as I chewed and swallowed it. Fun! It was like eating a drink. I was glad they weren't real frog eggs. "You can get this in the States now. They serve it in all different flavors of drinks and teas," Uncle Shin told us. "But it's called bubble tea or black pearl tea. 'Frog eggs' didn't sound appealing to Americans!"

We laughed, even though I thought it was a good name change. Frog eggs didn't sound appealing to me at all. I was American that way, too.

As we walked farther down, Uncle Shin said, "Ah! *Chou doufu!* Can you smell it?"

I sniffed the air. The only thing new that I smelled was an unpleasant odor that reminded me of the bathroom at the train station. Ki-Ki looked at me and pinched her nose, so I knew she smelled it, too. But we kept following Uncle Shin.

It was only when we met Grandpa, Grandma, Auntie Jin, and Uncle Flower in front of a food cart did I realize the smell was coming from there! I looked at the cart—nothing looked horrible. Silver trays full of golden fried squares of what I guessed was tofu. A woman, completely uncon-cerned by us, painted a brown sauce over them. Was it the food that smelled like that? I stood closer and sniffed...and then covered my nose and mouth! Yes, it was the food that smelled!

"What is that?" Lissy said, pinching her nose, too.

"*Chou doufu!*" Uncle Shin said. "Stinky tofu! It's famous!"

"Famous for smelling bad?" Lissy choked out.

"Yes," he laughed, "and for tasting delicious. You want one?"

chou doufu
(stinky tofu)

"No way!" I said. "It smells like throw-up!"

Everyone laughed. Grandpa, Grandma, Auntie Jin, and Uncle Flower stood to the side, all of them already eating from plates full of it. They seemed to really like it. And it looked like a lot of people did because as we stood there, person after person came up to the stall and bought some. None of them seemed disgusted.

"Here, try some of mine," Mom offered, holding up a piece of the tofu in her chopsticks.

Ki-Ki shook her head and clamped her lips tight. Lissy and I stared. It looked just like the fried tofu we'd had many times before. How could something that looked so harmless smell so bad?

"You try it," Lissy said to me.

"I don't want to try it!" I said. "You try it!"

"It's really good!" Aunt Bea said. "It's a Taiwan specialty. You shouldn't leave Taiwan without even trying it."

"I'll try it if you try it," Lissy said.

I hesitated. I had eaten raw fish and chicken feet. I should be able to eat some tofu, even if it did smell bad. "Okay," I said finally. "But you go first."

Lissy plugged her nose with her fingers again and reached for Mom's chopsticks. She took a deep breath, made a face like a squished lemon, and dropped the tofu into her mouth. And then swallowed. Everyone clapped and cheered as if she had just won a contest.

"Good for you!" Uncle Shin said. "See, pretty good, right? Now, Pacy, you try it!"

Lissy whispered to me, "I didn't really taste anything. I just swallowed it as fast as I could."

But now it was my turn. I pinched my nose like Lissy did, closed my eyes, carefully put the tofu in my mouth, and chewed. The tofu was soft with kind of a tangy taste that wasn't bad.... But I could still smell it! And in my mouth, it seemed to smell even stronger. I quickly swallowed.

"What did you think? Delicious, right?" Uncle Shin said as he ate his last piece. "I'm going to get some more. Do you want me to get you some?"

Lissy and I both shook our heads. I hoped no one else wanted more. I wanted to get away from the stinky tofu as soon as possible.

Chapter 31

Trouble

fortune-teller
at night market

EVERYONE FINALLY FINISHED EATING THE STINKY tofu, and we continued walking down the street. I was still hungry, but there was no food in the next part of the street. Instead, a row of red booths appeared. I watched as one of the peddlers tapped a gold disc that looked like a metal pancake with a chopstick. *Tap-tap-tap-*tap! The peddler hit it quickly, looking at a sheet of paper at the same time. Were they some sort of drum musicians? If they were, their music wasn't very good.

"Who are they?" I asked, rudely pointing.

"Fortune-tellers," Mom said, pushing my finger down.

More fortune-tellers! I was still surprised when I saw them. I kept thinking fortune-tellers would look more spooky or bizarre. These ones looked the same as Aunt Bea or Uncle Shin, wearing sweatshirts and glasses. I remembered the fortune-teller who had told my fortune, who had also looked so normal. She was the one who said I had a special skill that would stay with me. But my art talent had kept leaving in painting class, so she had been wrong about that. She also said I was going to get into trouble. Maybe she was wrong about that, too.

We passed the fortune-tellers, and then I saw lots of kids crowding around something in the middle of the street. Ki-Ki, Lissy, and I went over to see what was so interesting.

It was a big red plastic tub full of water. In the water, hundreds of goldfish swam and shimmered like shiny pennies.

"What are they for?" I asked.

"It's a game," Aunt Bea said. "You get a net and if you catch a goldfish, you can keep it."

the goldfish
game

"That's it?" Lissy said. "Some game!"

But the game was harder than it sounded. I watched as a pigtailed girl all dressed in red tried to catch a goldfish. She chased an orange fish with her net, trying over and over again to scoop it up. By the time she caught it, the net had crumbled and the fish easily escaped. It was only when she held up her tattered net and wailed did I realize that the nets were made out of paper.

"Can I try?" I asked.

No one answered me. I looked up and Mom, Lissy, Ki-Ki, Shogun, Uncle Shin — everyone — weren't there!

I was alone.

Chapter 32

Lost

photograph of
Dad's mother

I JUMPED UP. MAYBE I JUST HAD TO CATCH UP WITH them. But which way did they go? I couldn't remember which way we had walked from.

I followed the movement of the crowd. There were so many people, but none of them were Mom or Uncle Shin or Grandma or Grandpa. The night market was endless. Food, shopping, and games kept going and going. I kept walking aimlessly, wandering and looking.

Where were they? The longer I walked, the louder the noises grew in my ears. Where were they? Words I couldn't understand tripped and ran into each other over and on top of me. The smoke and smells flooded the air, and the neon signs glared with their garish colors. Where were they? The black sky seemed to come alive, and I felt like I was getting pressed into the mouth of a giant monster. The bright demon-colored red of the fortune-tellers' booths reappeared and the *tap-tap-tapping* of the sticks echoed my heartbeat. Where were they? Where were they? Where were they? I started walking faster and faster. And suddenly, like a stabbing knife, fear cut into me. Where was I?

I was lost. That first fortune-teller had been right. I was in trouble, big trouble.

People swarmed and shoved, walking as if they didn't see me. As if I were invisible to them. The burning air filled my lungs, and I gasped to breathe. I was the tree that no one saw, that didn't exist. I was erased; somehow a ghost had gotten me, and now I was a ghost, too. A hungry ghost, desperate and scared, that no one could see and no one cared about. A sick, nauseous feeling formed at the bottom of my throat. I didn't belong here! This place with the meaningless words and the harsh lights was fading me away. Soon, I'd be gone, evaporating into nothingness. I was going to disappear.

All of the sudden, someone grabbed my arm. I almost screamed, but then I saw it was Shogun.

"Pacy?" he said, and then he said a lot of words in Chinese I didn't understand. But I didn't care. I was so glad to see him! Tears started to pour out of my eyes, and my breath

Shogun when he found me

started to hiccup. Shogun tightened his hand on my arm and pulled me down the street.

Then I saw Mom and Auntie Jin and Aunt Bea, Lissy and Ki-Ki. Seeing all of them again, their familiar faces after being so scared—I cried even harder. Mom hugged me tight and Auntie Jin and Aunt Bea joined in, too. Even Lissy and Ki-Ki were relieved.

"Where were you?" Lissy said. "Everyone is looking for you!"

"You're supposed to stay in one place when you get lost," Aunt Bea said, "so people can find you!"

"Grandma and Grandpa went home, just in case you gave your name card to someone and they brought you there," Auntie Jin said, her words streaming over Aunt Bea's.

I tried to stop crying, but I couldn't. I knew I was too old to cry like this, but the tears flooded from my eyes like an overflowing pot. I hadn't thought about staying in one place or my name card. I had been so scared, I hadn't thought about anything and I still couldn't. All I knew was that I didn't want to be there anymore. I didn't want to be in Taiwan. I wanted to be back in New Hartford, back where I knew where everything was and understood everything and I wasn't a ghost. "I want to go home!" I sobbed.

Mom looked over me at Aunt Bea. "I'll take her back," Mom said. "The rest of you can stay."

Mom held my hand tightly through the crowds, even though it was all wet and slobbery. When we got to the main street out

mom holding
my hand as we
left the night
market

of the night market, instead of going toward the subway, she
raised her arm for a taxi. As we got in, she took out a new
change purse, green this time, and handed me some tissues.

Seeing Mom's new change purse reminded me about how
she was a visiting ghost, too. Her home was New Hartford,
just like mine. But this used to be her home. She and Dad
chose to become ghosts. In a way, they made us ghosts.

"Why did you and Dad move to America?" I said after
blowing my nose.

Mom was quiet for a moment, and I thought she didn't
hear me. But suddenly she said, "When we left, things
weren't good in Taiwan. There was martial law then."

"What's martial law?" I asked.

"It's when the government is scared and so mistrustful that they are very strict and suspicious with the people," Mom said. "Sometimes they are so strict that they are cruel. We wanted to get away from that."

"What do you mean?" I asked.

"Remember Big Uncle?" Mom said. "The government was cruel to him."

WHEN BIG UNCLE WAS ARRESTED

When Dad was a young boy, Dad's oldest brother — Big Uncle — was the one who supported the whole family. Big Uncle wasn't much older than a boy himself, but he was smart and hardworking; the five brothers, two sisters, the parents, and the grandparents all survived mostly on Big Uncle's salary as a schoolteacher.

But late one night, there was a loud bang on the door, like the sound of arriving thunder. It was the military police! They had some questions they wanted to ask Big Uncle, they said, and they put him in a jeep and disappeared.

The family didn't know what to do. They didn't know where he was, what happened, or why. But they knew the military police were always secretive and always serious. The next day, Dad's mother gathered all the jewelry and money in the house and went from one official to the next, bribing them for information about Big Uncle.

It was a hard time. As the news was whispered that Big Uncle had been taken for political reasons, everyone was afraid. Friends and relatives stayed away. It was almost like Dad's family had become poison. No one wanted to be connected to Dad's family because then they, too, might be arrested. And without Big Uncle's salary, the family was so poor. They even had to beg for scraps to feed their pig. Days and months passed, and you can't even imagine how poor they became. They had to make horrible choices. Sad choices. When Dad's mother had a new baby girl, her mother-in-law forced her to give up the baby to be adopted.

Then, almost two years later, there was another late-night noise at the door. This time it was a single soft knock, tired and resigned. Only Dad heard it, and when he opened the door – there was Big Uncle!

He was in rags and looked like a starving beggar. But it was only then that they found out why he had been arrested. A vice principal at Big Uncle's school had a scholar friend who had been caught with a book on Communism. Because of that, any friends of the scholar and anyone associated with those friends had been arrested. Luckily for Big Uncle, some of those people had connections with the government and were able to get the charges for the whole group overturned, which was why Big Uncle could finally come home.

But even after Big Uncle came home, things weren't easy. He had been cleared of the charges, but people were still afraid

207

to be connected to him. His reputation was damaged. People looked at Big Uncle as if he were a dangerous bomb. He couldn't teach at his school—or any school—anymore. It was hard to find a job. It was hard to find friends.

"That's why," Mom continued, "when Dad got the opportunity to go work in America, his family said, 'Go! Go!' They knew it would take him far away, but they wanted him to be in a place where things that happened to Big Uncle could not happen to him."

"I didn't know Dad had a younger sister," I said.

"They try not to talk about her," Mom said. "They were ashamed they couldn't keep her, and I remember if she ever came up in conversation, Dad's mom would cry."

I realized the baby girl was my aunt, an aunt I would never know. I remembered the photo of Dad's mom on our wall back home, her serious eyes staring out. Those were the hungry ghosts, I thought. Sad memories and bad memories were those ghosts that haunted. When Dad's mom was getting her photo taken, there had been ghosts around her. Dad and Big Uncle had ghosts around them, too. Everyone did. Even I had ghosts, not as bad as Big Uncle's, but smaller ones like the mean bus driver and the horrible girls who called me Twinkie and the angry woman at the market in Taichung. Those were the ghosts that always came back, no matter what you did to try to keep them away.

But I thought about Big Uncle and how even though his face looked tired, it still wrinkled into a big smile and his laugh was deep and hearty. I thought about Dad being a young boy, poor and hungry, and then how now he could eat. "The best!" he had said with his eyes sparkling. Those ghosts hadn't stopped them from being alive and happy. They had learned to live with their ghosts. And I could, too.

Chapter 33

Found

dinner back home

GRANDMA AND GRANDPA WERE WAITING, JUST LIKE Auntie Jin said they would be. When they heard our steps climbing the stairs, they threw open the door and sighed as if they hadn't breathed all day. When we reached them, they both hugged me tight, and a few more tears crept down my face. It was just so nice to be there, in the kitchen with the round table I ate at in the morning and sofa that I sat on. When I had said I wanted to go home, I had meant New Hartford, but being here felt good. I realized that being here felt like home, too.

Mom gave me a warm cloth to wash my face, and Grandpa poured me a glass of sugarcane juice. I had just finished my second cup and was feeling better when we heard the familiar pounding up the stairs. As the door opened, everyone came in, looked at me, and smiled broad grins.

"Better?" Auntie Jin and Aunt Bea asked as they patted my shoulders. "Good," Uncle Shin said, giving me a hug. Uncle Flower rubbed me on the head. "Pacy, glad we found you. Glad you are okay."

"I thought you'd stay a lot longer at the night market," Mom said. "We've only been back a little while."

"We did stay for a bit," Uncle Shin said. "But we didn't think it was as much fun without you there, so we decided to come back."

"I won a goldfish!" Ki-Ki said, thrusting a plastic bag full of water and a googly-eyed orange fish at me. "We can share if you want."

goldfish that
Lissy and Ki-Ki won

"No, I won two," Lissy said, dangling her bag with a silver and a black fish in it. "You can have one of mine."

"Did you know," Ki-Ki said, "you can get a kitten or a puppy from a vending machine at the night market? Really! We wanted to get one for you—well, really, for all of us—but Uncle Shin wouldn't let us."

"Good!" Mom said.

"But we brought home a lot of food," Aunt Bea said. "Just in case you didn't get enough."

All the fear I had at the night market was melting away, like ice in front of a warm fire. I felt embarrassed about crying so much and being such a baby about getting lost, but I kind of liked how everyone was being so nice to me. Auntie

Jin got a bowl for our goldfish, and we dropped them in. Lissy said I could choose which fish I wanted, but I knew she wanted the black one and was just being nice. So, to be nice back, I took the silver one.

Aunt Bea and Mom unpacked the food. There was a lot of it—deep-fried golden cubes, pancake-looking bread with green onions, copper-colored rolls of something, meat in brown sauce on rice, a carton of green vegetables cooked with garlic, and fat-fried chicken wings. "These are special," Uncle Shin said as he displayed the wings. "There are no bones in these. They take out the bones and then stuff the wings with fried rice and egg yolks."

chicken wings stuffed with rice and egg

"This isn't all for me, is it?" I asked, looking at all the food. "I'm not that hungry!"

"We didn't know what you would like," Uncle Flower said. "So we let Lissy and Ki-Ki pick a little bit from every stall, too."

"You're lucky we chose," Lissy said, "or else you'd be stuck with more stinky tofu. They make it grilled and fried, and Uncle Shin thought you might want to try both."

Everyone laughed at that, but I was grateful. Just the smell of that tofu would have ruined the rest of the food.

"Well," Mom said, "I don't think Pacy can eat everything, so why don't we all have a second dinner?"

"We should do this every night!" Uncle Shin said, and then

he stopped and gave a wry smile. "I meant the second dinner every night. Not Pacy getting lost."

"Yes, not that," Uncle Flower said, and looked at me. "That was terrible, not knowing where you were. We thought you had disappeared."

I shivered. I had thought I had disappeared, too. But I hadn't. I was still here, and I was glad.

"Hey," Ki-Ki said. "Where's the big one?"

"Oh, the special one!" Auntie Jin said. She looked around and then picked up a plastic bag Shogun had left on the chair. She took out a big carton and opened it on the table. A warm, savory smell drifted out, and I knew right away what they were.

"Dumplings!" I said.

jiaozi
(dumplings)

Everyone laughed, and I joined in. But sitting at the table, I remembered how I had sat there on the first day of painting class and said to Mom, "I don't want to know who I am, then!" That wasn't true. I did want to know who I was. I had thought of myself as a lot of different things here in Taiwan — a Twinkie, a ghost, an artist—and I hadn't felt that my Chinese name fit. But as I looked around the table at everyone, with their faces smiling at me, I felt safe and treasured. I guessed I was a precious thought, after all.

Chapter 34

The Exhibit

Ki-Ki's paper cut

FOUR DAYS LATER, LISSY, KI-KI, AND I WERE GETTING ready for the exhibit. Grandma said we should look nice, since we were the artists. At first I thought that meant I had to wear my special Chinese dress, but Mom said to save that for Grandma's party. So I just wore my strawberry dress again.

Grandma, Aunt Bea, Auntie Jin, and Uncle Shin came, too. Grandpa wanted to come, but he had to work. The exhibit was in the same building we had our classes in, but on a different floor. It was new to have so many people in the elevator with us. It felt unfamiliar pressing the number five instead of the other three numbers we were used to, and when the elevator doors opened, the floor was really different, too.

Instead of a hall of classrooms, there was a glass wall on one side with clean Chinese writing on it. I think it probably said GALLERY on it, because I could see it was like a museum inside.

Pictures hung on the wall under spotlights, little sculptures stood on blocks, and the floor was shiny and polished. I felt a little awed and unsure if we should enter. But I thought I saw Alex and Eva from my class in the gallery, so we went in.

Everything looked so good, like real artists had done it. One wall had all the work from Lissy's class. About twenty scrolls hung next to each other, each painting mounted on red silk with a dragon pattern on it.

"Which one is yours?" Mom asked Lissy.

Lissy walked down the length of the room. "Here it is," she said, stopping in the middle.

To me, it looked just like everyone else's but with different characters. Well, the brush strokes were thicker. Lissy's painting had only one character, so the marks were thick. The scroll to the right of hers had a whole line of characters that looked like a map of dance directions.

"What does it say?" I asked her.

"'Happiness,'" she said. I looked closer. I had stamped "happiness" on my painting using my teacher's chop, but I didn't remember the character looking like that. Maybe I was remembering wrong.

"Mine is over here!" Ki-Ki said, pulling at us.

Lissy's "happiness" calligraphy

215

The paper cuts in Ki-Ki's class weren't mounted on scrolls but were instead framed under glass. If the teacher hadn't given us the talk about mounting the paintings, I would've thought it was kind of cheap that we didn't get ours framed, too. Anyway, the paper cuts were a lot smaller, so they were probably cheaper to frame.

Ki-Ki pointed at a red paper cut on the wall. It was like a snowflake, but it had intricate flowers and leaves radiating out of a center star. I was really impressed.

"Did you really do that?" Lissy asked. She was impressed, too.

Ki-Ki nodded. We all crowded around it.

"So good, Ki-Ki!" Uncle Shin said. "Was it hard to do?"

"No," Ki-Ki said, shaking her head. "But it took a lot of time. Especially cutting the little pieces."

I was feeling a little jealous. Where was my painting? The work from my class had to be somewhere. I looked around and saw a row of olive-green scrolls on the wall in the other room. Those must be ours.

I left everyone with Ki-Ki's paper cut and walked over to the scrolls. Yes, they were my class's. Mounting the paintings did make them look finished. The brownish-green silk had a subtle, small leaf pattern all over it. I was glad it wasn't red, like Lissy's, because I didn't think red would look good with my pink birds. And there they were! Right at the end, next to Audrey Chiang's painting.

I felt proud when I saw my painting. Somehow, the mounting had made the colors more delicate-looking, and the sheen of the silk seemed to make my painting glow, too. I glanced over at Audrey's. Hers looked better, too. I worked hard not to glare at it.

Lissy came over to me, holding something in a napkin.

"There are refreshments!" she told me. "Just soda and different kinds of cookies, though."

She stopped in front of the paintings. "Which one's yours?" she asked, cocking her head. I pointed. I didn't tell her that the three birds were supposed to me, her, and Ki-Ki. She might think that was stupid and laugh.

"Huh," she said. Then she squinted close. "What does the chop say?"

"'Happiness,'" I told her.

"No, it doesn't!" she said. "I should know. I had to paint that character a hundred times."

"*Happiness* is what the paper said," I insisted. "Maybe it's just another Chinese word for 'happiness.'"

Uncle Shin, Mom, and Ki-Ki came over. Uncle Shin and Mom had cookies in their hands, and Ki-Ki had cookie on her face.

"This one is yours?" Mom asked. "Very good!" Uncle Shin nodded in agreement.

"But that doesn't say *happiness*, does it?" Lissy said, pointing at my chop mark.

"Hmm," Uncle Shin peered close so that his nose almost

touched the paper. "No. It says, um, how do you say it... 'unchangeable', 'permanent.'"

"'Unchangeable'?" I said. I didn't even remember that being a choice.

"More like 'lasting,'" Mom said. "'Forever.'"

Forever? Oh no, someone must have mixed the teacher's chops up, and I had used the *forever* one. That made no sense with my painting! Why would three birds wish for forever? Why would Lissy, Ki-Ki, and I wish for that?

"forever" stamp

Then I saw Audrey Chiang. She was wearing a dark purple dress with black buttons. She was walking to her painting, which meant toward us, with a tall, thin lady with short hair. I guessed she was her mother.

Audrey nodded at me, and the woman said something in Chinese, probably asking if Audrey knew us. Audrey nodded again, and the woman smiled at us.

"*Ni hao, ni hao,*" she said, and then she said something to me in Chinese. I tried to guess what she was saying. Either she was asking if I was in Audrey's class or which painting was mine. Or maybe she was asking if I liked painting. I had no idea. So I just shook my head.

"*Bu hui shuo Hanyu,*" Mom jumped in. I could figure out what Mom said there! *She can't speak Chinese.*

"Bu hui shuo!" the woman said. I knew that, too. *Can't speak Chinese!* Her eyes widened as if Mom had said

meeting Audrey's mother

something horrible, and she looked at me as if I had suddenly turned into a purple worm. She was definitely Audrey's mother.

The woman said some more words in Chinese to Mom. I couldn't figure those out, but Mom looked embarrassed and shook her head. Again! I wanted to let out a big sigh. The same heavy, discouraged feeling draped over me, like it always did when this happened. I glanced at Audrey, expecting to see a mirror of her mother's scorn.

But when I looked up, Audrey looked...sorry? She looked

uncomfortable, as if she thought her mother's words were rude. Her eyes met mine, and she gave me a small, rueful smile.

I was confused. Maybe Audrey wasn't that bad? I wasn't sure, but suddenly I didn't hate her completely. I still wanted my painting to beat hers, though. Then Mom and Audrey's mother stopped talking, and Audrey and her mother walked away.

"What did she say?" I asked.

"Oh, nothing important, hello and where do you live," Mom said. "Those kind of things."

"No, the part where you were talking about me," I said.

"She was surprised that you didn't know Chinese and couldn't believe I didn't teach you," Mom said. "Is her daughter your friend?"

"Not really," I said. Audrey was more like my enemy. But now I was more interested in what Audrey's mother had said. It sounded like she thought it was Mom's fault I didn't know Chinese. I wonder if Mom felt as bad as I did when people thought I was a Twinkie.

"Do you wish you taught us Chinese?" I asked Mom.

Mom stopped and thought seriously. "Yes," Mom said. "Sometimes, I regret I didn't teach all of you when you were younger. But I can't change that now. And just because you don't know the language doesn't mean you are not Taiwanese."

"But I'm not Taiwanese," I said. "I'm American."

"You're Taiwanese-American," Mom said. "And, no matter what, that's what you'll always be."

Forever, I thought. I'd always be Taiwanese-American, no matter if I spoke Chinese, made my eyes bigger, or was called a Twinkie. Even if I didn't like it. Being Taiwanese-American was like making a brush stroke. The mark couldn't be erased, and the ink and the paper could never be separated. They were joined forever.

"Mom!" I said, grabbing her arm before she walked away. "For my name chop, can I have my name carved in Chinese and English? Can they do that?"

"Yes." Mom nodded, a little surprised. "I'm sure they can. I'll order them today."

"Good," I said, and I felt as if I had just taken off a winter coat after discovering it was summer. I was glad I had found my identity.

Chapter 35

Being the Best

Eva Wong happy
after winning

I WAS SO HAPPY ABOUT FIGURING OUT MY NAME CHOP that I almost forgot about the ribbons for the best class painting. Audrey Chiang hadn't forgotten, though. As I stood by the refreshment table, trying to decide between an almond cookie and a buttery, lacy-looking one, she came by and hissed, "They're giving the prizes now!"

"They" were all the teachers, five of them together in a group. I recognized my teacher — he had a clipboard in his hand. An older lady with a yellow rose pinned to her bright orange shirt carried the prize ribbons in her hands. They were blue, and, against her shirt, they seemed to glow.

They were walking to each wall, looking at the list on the clipboard, and then pinning a ribbon next to the winning art. Everyone began to follow them. It felt like a circus parade. When a teacher in a green dress pinned a ribbon onto a rose embroidery, everyone clapped and shouted.

Lissy's class was next, and the blue ribbon went to one that had two columns of words up and down the paper. Lissy didn't seem that disappointed. She just smiled and clapped, and we kept following the teachers. They were heading over to the paper cuts. One of the younger teachers walked over with a blue ribbon and pinned it onto Ki-Ki's paper cut! Ki-Ki had won a ribbon!

Uncle Shin, Lissy, and I whooped, and Mom and Aunt Bea clapped so hard that I could see their hands turning red. Ki-Ki beamed a thousand smiles. I quickly scanned the rest of the paper cuts. Hers was the best. She deserved it. I felt proud.

But I couldn't pay any more attention, because now they were walking over to my class's paintings. We were the last group, I guess because our work was on the farthest wall. Audrey Chiang watched, unsmiling, just staring at the group as if trying to hypnotize them. My hands went cold, and the cookie I had eaten seemed to be stuck in my throat.

The lady in orange handed my teacher the last blue ribbon. He looked around at all of us and smiled. He checked his clipboard and walked down toward Audrey's painting and mine. Which one would it be? Would I beat Audrey?

No. The teacher walked by both mine and Audrey's and pinned the ribbon on a painting of two birds flying under a flowering branch. I hadn't painted that. Neither had Audrey. A squeal of happiness came from the audience, and I saw Eva jump up and down in happiness. I hadn't won. Each one of Eva's hops seemed to flatten me, like a teddy bear losing its stuffing. My eyes stung with disappointment, but I was able to blink it away and clap politely. At least Audrey hadn't beaten me.

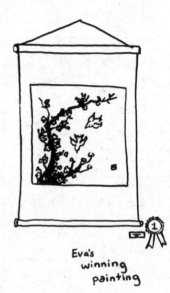

Eva's winning painting

I looked at her. She was clapping politely, too, but the smile on her face looked more like she was clenching her teeth. She looked like a cat ready to attack.

The crowd began to spread out, and I walked over to Lissy, Aunt Bea, and Uncle Shin. Grandma, Auntie Jin, and Mom were taking photos of Ki-Ki by her winning paper cut. I felt better seeing Ki-Ki grin. It made sense that Ki-Ki would win. Her name meant "victorious thought." Besides, Lissy hadn't won, either.

Grandma & Mom
taking a photo of Ki-Ki

"I just want to know what I could've done to make my painting better." Audrey's voice carried over to us, and we all looked over. Audrey was questioning our teacher like he was a spy. Her mother was standing behind her, nodding.

"That girl is weird," Lissy said. Then she pretended she was talking to Audrey. "Your painting wasn't the best. Get over it already."

"Maybe she just wants to know how she can improve," Aunt Bea said. "That's always good."

"No." I shook my head. "She just wanted to win."

"I know people like that. Some people are only happy when they are first or the best," Uncle Shin said, and then he looked at us with a playful grin. "But, for me, that's no fun."

"Pacy," Grandma said. "Let's take a photo of you by your painting."

"But I didn't win!" I said.

"I still love it," Grandma said. "I think it's beautiful."

"Yes! Your painting is still good anyway!" Auntie Jin said. "Go stand by it!"

"And smile!" Mom said.

I followed their orders. Grandma, Mom, and Auntie Jin clicked away at their cameras and then pushed Lissy toward her painting. As I turned around, I saw Eva by her painting.

"Congratulations," I said. I was still a little jealous, but I tried not to let it show. I looked at her painting. The brown birds were soft and graceful, and the flowers had fine, delicate heart-shaped petals. It was a really good painting. I still kind of liked mine better, but I could see why hers had won a ribbon. I wondered why I had never really paid that much attention to Eva or her paintings before. I guessed it was because I was so busy watching Audrey.

"Thanks!" Eva said. She was bubbling over with happiness. "I just loved painting class! I can't believe it's over. I'm going to miss it. The class was so much fun, don't you think?"

I smiled at her, but I was surprised. Painting class, fun? I thought about all the days I spent there, gritting my teeth at Audrey and trying to force my art talent to paint better. It hadn't been fun for me.

And then I realized I was more like Uncle Shin than I was like Audrey. If my painting had won tonight, I would've been really happy. But when Clifford had us pick the four best pleasures in life, being the best hadn't even come to my mind. Maybe it wasn't that Audrey was so horrible; maybe it was just that trying to be better than everyone else was what she thought was fun, the only thing that made her happy. But it wasn't for me. Winning was fun, but it wasn't the only thing that made me happy.

"I really liked your painting," Eva said. "I thought all your paintings in class were nice."

"Thanks," I said. Eva's big smile reminded me of Melody's. "What chop did you use?"

"Well, I meant to use the chop that said 'profundity,' because it sounded good, even though I don't know what it means," Eva said. "But my mom told me that the stamp says 'spring'!"

"That happened to me, too!" I said. "I thought I was stamping 'happiness,' but I got 'forever'!"

"Someone must have mixed up all the stamps," she said.

"What does *profundity* mean, anyway?" I asked.

"I still don't know," Eva said. We looked at each other, and we both burst out laughing. Why had I been so caught up with Audrey? I should've talked to Eva before.

"Eva! We have to go!" a woman, probably Eva's mom, called.

227

"I better go," she said. "Good-bye."

"Good-bye," I said, and I felt sad. Why had I wasted all those days of class, making myself unhappy, trying to beat Audrey? Instead, I could've become friends with Eva, and it would've been fun. Instead of dreading painting class, I could've loved it just like Eva did. And maybe Eva and I could've become really good friends like me and Melody. But now it was too late. I probably wouldn't see Eva again.

"In Chinese painting," the teacher had said, "you can't take back anything you do." I guessed that was true in real life, too. But I wished it wasn't.

Chapter 36

Four Days Left

Grandma's
corsage

ALL THE DAYS WERE RUSHING BY. LIKE A TRAIN, TIME WAS
moving faster and faster. There were only six days left here
in Taiwan, then five, and now four. The crowds, busyness,
and dirtiness of the city didn't bother me so much anymore.
I didn't feel scared about how everything was so different
than in New Hartford. Of course, I still didn't like it when
shopkeepers looked at me strangely because I didn't speak
Chinese—though, when I thought about it, sometimes the
shopkeepers in New Hartford gave me the same strange look.

But I had gotten used to eating big meals and laughing
even when I didn't know what was funny. I liked going to the
street market and choosing wax apples and munching them
on the way home. It was those everyday things that happened
over and over again that I couldn't imagine ending. But they
would, once we left Taiwan. Our time here was running out.

eating a wax
apple & walking

Tomorrow was Grandma's party, and we would be leaving two days later. I was excited about Grandma's party, but it was odd to think we would be leaving so soon. Aunt Yoko, Uncle Sam, baby Sylvia, and Auntie Kim were in Taiwan now, too, and everyone was busy doing things—talking on the phone, ordering things, and getting special dresses dry-cleaned. Uncle Flower, Julian, Shogun, and their father were always hiding someplace to practice their "secret." I really wanted to know what the surprise was. Lissy said she thought they were going to put on a play or sing a song. But I didn't know why that would have to be a secret.

The main room in Grandpa's place felt like a flower shop, full of colors and sweet smells. Bouquets of flowers had been delivered, big pink flowers with feathery ferns. A wreath made of flowers came, too. We weren't sure if they were gifts or things ordered for the party.

The only thing we were sure of for the party was a clear plastic box that held a regal purple orchid decorated with a sheer lavender ribbon and ferns. "Grandma's corsage," Mom said, and she put it in the refrigerator. It was funny to see it next to the eggs and juice.

"I hope when I turn sixty, people have a big party for me," Lissy said.

"Me, too," I said. But I couldn't really imagine turning sixty years old. It seemed so far away and unreal and...old! "You really deserve a party when you're sixty."

"Uh-huh." Ki-Ki nodded. "Because you're so old then!"

Uncle Flower was on his way out to go practice "the secret" but stopped when he heard us. "Is sixty so old?" he said, laughing.

We nodded.

"Well, an old emperor agreed with you," he said. "It's another reason why we celebrate a person's sixtieth birthday."

THE VALUE OF ELDERS

Once, there was a young emperor who didn't believe his elders held much wisdom. In fact, he felt as soon as they reached the age of sixty, they became useless and were simply a burden to the state and family. Convinced of this, he made a decree that once a person reached the age of sixty, he or she would be executed.

The emperor had an adviser who not only did not agree with this, but also had a father (to whom he went to for all advice) who was about to turn sixty years old. "I can't let my father be executed!" he said to himself. But what to do? Finally he decided to hide his father in a mountain cave, bringing him food every day.

The adviser soon had other worries, as well. A neighboring state

constantly clashed with the emperor's kingdom, and a war seemed inevitable. So it was a great surprise when one day an emissary from the state arrived seeking an audience with the emperor. At his visit, the emissary brought out two pieces of rough wood. They looked exactly alike and were the same shape and thickness.

"These pieces of wood are from the same tree. One is from the branch and the other from the root," the emissary said. "If you can tell me which is from the root and which is from the branch, our state will cede our authority to you."

The emperor could not tell the difference. Neither could any of the court officials or advisers. The emperor offered a reward throughout his kingdom, yet no one stepped forward. The neighboring state began to grow restless, and war loomed closer and closer.

emissary with two pieces of wood

When the adviser brought his hidden father food that day, the father couldn't help noticing his son's worried face.

"What is it?" he asked.

The adviser told his father about the emissary's visit. "How can one tell the difference between wood from a branch and wood from a root?" he said.

His father laughed. "Ho, ho, quite easily," he said. "Put them both in water. The root will sink, and the branch will float."

The adviser hurried away and did as his father told him. It was true! The emperor solved the state's riddle, and both sides put down their arms. War was averted! There was great rejoicing.

"You are a brilliant man! I will reward you well!" the emperor said to his adviser. "How did you find the solution?"

The adviser kowtowed low. "I did not find the solution myself. It was my father and his wisdom and experience that told me. For my reward, I ask that you spare him execution for his age."

The emperor was astounded. "Your father?" he said, and then after much thought, "I have thought that the old are useless and foolish. However, it was only an elder's wisdom and experience that prevented war. I was wrong."

The next day, the emperor took back his decree of execution for all elders. The adviser brought his father back from the mountains, and the emperor held a grand celebration in the old man's honor. Coincidentally, it was also his sixtieth birthday.

"And that became a tradition," Uncle Flower said. "That's why we are making Grandma's birthday party so big, with all the flowers, food —"

"And your secret?" I interrupted.

"Yes!" Uncle Flower said, smiling. "We want to make sure this is a big and special celebration. The emperor, so long ago, honored the sixtieth birthday, so we try to do the same."

"Yeah," I said. "Because it's so old."

Uncle Flower sighed.

Chapter 37

Gift for Grandma

GRACE PACY

mark that
my name chop
made

WHEN UNCLE FLOWER LEFT, I LOOKED AT LISSY AND
Ki-Ki. "We're the only ones not doing anything for Grandma's party," I said.

"Well, it's not like we can help with anything," Lissy said.
"We can't speak Chinese, and we don't know where anything is."

That was true.

"We should give Grandma a birthday present!" Ki-Ki said.
"You have to give a present at a birthday!"

"I don't think we have time to go shopping for a birthday present," Mom told us. "Today, we have to pick up your
art from the exhibit, your name chops, and Lissy's photos. If
there is time afterward, we can try."

But there wasn't any time afterward. On the subway,
even as Lissy enjoyed the glory of her album, I fingered the

my finished
name chop

smooth stone of my carved name chop, and Ki-Ki clutched her blue ribbon, we felt ashamed. We had been in Taiwan for twenty-four days and had known about Grandma's party the whole time, yet we didn't have a single birthday gift. That was pretty bad.

"Grandma won't care if you don't give her anything," Mom said. "But if you really want to give her something, she wouldn't want a gift from the store anyway. You should make her something or give her something that is really from you."

I thought hard as the subway screeched to a stop and we all walked back home. The sun was setting, and the sky looked as if bright

feeling ashamed on subway

pink and orange paint had been spilled on it. We were going to be flying home in that sky soon. I wished I could slow down time.

235

After we got inside, I ran for some scrap paper. I was eager to try out my chop. I plied open the shallow, round tin of ink that we had bought for the chops. The ink was vivid red and sticky like paste. With a firm grip, I rubbed my chop in the tin, making sure the whole surface was covered with ink. Then, as hard as I dared, I stamped the paper. *Clunk!* Carefully, I lifted it, gently holding down the paper as it tried to stick. There it was.

I looked at it with satisfaction. It seemed to look back at me cheerfully. The crisp red square, the Chinese characters, and GRACE PACY in block letters. Should I have gotten *Grace Pacy Lin*, since that was my whole name in English? Hmm. Well, some of the Chinese characters meant *Lin*, but none meant *Grace*. So maybe it was okay. Maybe it made things kind of equal. *Grace* was the part of me that was all American, *Lin* was the part that was all Asian, but *Pacy* was both. Besides, *Grace Pacy Lin* probably wouldn't have fit. *Grace Pacy* looked a little squished to me already.

I gently rubbed it with my finger. The ink had dried already, not a line smeared. Anyway, on the paper, my mark, my identity, was forever.

I took out my painting from the exhibit. I rolled it out, the heavy, stiff silk felt rich against my fingers. The pink birds looked happy sitting on their bamboo, their colors delicate and vivid at the same time. I was kind of surprised that I still liked it. Because it hadn't won the ribbon, I thought maybe it wasn't any good. But I had thought it was good before Eva won the ribbon and the painting hadn't changed at all. Just because it hadn't won, why should I think any different about it now? And even if Audrey had been a better painter than me sometimes, I was still an artist. My talent was forever, too. I had thought it had kept disappearing, but it was still there. I just hadn't been looking at it the right way.

The pink birds were on bamboo. When you painted bamboo, that meant you were wishing something, I remembered. What were the birds wishing? I had never figured that out. If the birds were me, Lissy, and Ki-Ki, then maybe we were wishing Grandma a happy birthday. Grandma had said she loved my painting. I decided I'd give it to her.

But it wasn't finished yet. I rubbed my chop in the red paste again, over and over again, double the number of times I did before. I wanted this chop mark to be perfect. I took a deep breath and carefully centered my hand where I wanted the mark to be. *Clunk!* I stamped.

my finished
painting

I was almost afraid to lift the chop to see the mark. What if I had ruined the whole painting? But I carefully lifted it. Perfect!

I sat back and looked at the whole painting. The three birds, the "forever" mark, and my name. The tiger on my chop grinned at me. The painting was perfect. It was the perfect gift for Grandma. Now Grandma's birthday party could come!

Chapter 38

Grandma
all dressed up
for the party

WHEN WE WOKE UP THE NEXT MORNING, IT SEEMED like the day was already at full speed. I had said that Lissy, Ki-Ki, and I had nothing to do for Grandma's party, but even we were rushing and running around. It was like we were trying to catch Grandma's party in a chase.

"If you have a gift for Grandma, put it in this bag," Aunt Bea said. She and Auntie Jin were leaving before us to get the restaurant ready. "We'll bring it for the gift table."

I put my rolled-up painting in the bag, and Mom pushed me to get ready. We had to get all dressed up in our fancy Chinese dresses. I remembered that when we packed them, I had thought we would be wearing them all the time, since they were our only Chinese clothes. But this was the first time we were wearing them all summer. Part of all the busyness and hurrying around had been to get our clothes to fit. Mom had made us try them on in the morning, and they had all been too tight. In mine, I had felt like a bulging caterpillar trapped in a cocoon, and Lissy's dress wouldn't even zip up.

Grandma fixing my dress

Mom was going to run out and buy us new ones, but Grandma had shook her head. Instead, Grandma turned all the dresses inside out and took out stitches and resewed them. Now my silk dress wasn't tight anywhere, except for at the collar. But it had always been tight there; that was just the way Chinese dresses were.

I was really disappointed that we didn't get new dresses. I had never liked my dress, anyway. I was still wearing the frog-green one that Lissy outgrew. As I buttoned the smooth silk collar, I saw there were small Chinese symbols embroidered on it. I had never paid attention to them before, but now I saw one was a character I had seen before. Which one was it?

"What does this mean again?" I asked Mom, pointing at the symbol. "Is it 'forever'?"

"No," Mom said, "This one is 'happiness,' remember? They usually put the word for 'happiness' on clothes for kids and 'long life' on clothes for adults."

Happiness. Like Lissy's painting. "Long life" must have been the symbol that was on Grandma's dress, then. Grandma wore a dress the rich color of the fine, polished, red-stained wood-carving and a green jade bracelet and button-shaped earrings. Mom pinned the large purple orchid near Grandma's collar. I wondered if it was still cold from being in the refrigerator.

me in my
fancy Chinese dress

At the restaurant, there were already people waiting. Grandma's party was in a private room in the back, and when she and Grandpa entered, a great cheer went up. But I didn't really hear it, because I was looking at everything. No wonder Aunt Bea and Auntie Jin had left early. They had had a lot to do. At every dinner table, there was a vase of flowers, and on each of the chairs was a box holding a decorated rice bowl. The bowls were deep pink with a design of curlicue flowers surrounding the Chinese long-life symbol (which I now knew). Mom said they were party favors for the guests.

On the side, there was a gift table that was covered with presents. I didn't see my painting there, but maybe it was underneath. There were so many gifts! Some of them weren't wrapped, and we could see that they were gold Chinese symbols mounted on red velvet or silk and framed. I saw a long-life symbol in the pile. All the gifts looked expensive. I wondered if the symbols were made of real gold.

A table with a bright red silk cloth was right by the door with some black markers.

Uncle Shin
signing the red fabric

"Here, sign your name," Uncle Shin told us.

"Why?" I asked.

"It's kind of a guest book," he told us, "but Chinese style."

The cloth was already marked with black signatures and Chinese symbols. I thought it ruined the cloth, which was smooth, shiny silk. It could've been made into a beautiful dress or shirt if it hadn't been messed up by all the markers. But since it was already spoiled, I wrote my name in the corner. I wrote it in English and Chinese, just like my chop, though I wasn't completely sure if I got all my Chinese name right.

Aunt Bea came up to Uncle Shin and talked to him in Taiwanese.

"Time for me to be the master!" he joked at us before he strode away to the middle of the room. "Master of the ceremony, I mean."

And after clinking his wineglass with a fork, Uncle Shin began to make a speech to everyone in the room. It was in Taiwanese, of course, so I didn't know what he was saying. But Grandma and Grandpa looked happy and proud standing next to him. People laughed and clapped at different times until finally Uncle Shin said something very loudly. This made everyone clap even louder, and then people started to move. Mom pushed us toward the dinner tables. It was time to eat!

Chapter 39

Lots of Gifts

red envelope
with money

FOOD WAS PLACED ON THE TABLE IN A RUSH. AS SOON as we sat down, the waiters almost threw down a big bowl of thick, silvery soup; a platter of shrimp with nuts that looked as if they were candy-coated; a golden roasted chicken already sliced into bite-size pieces; a dark brown duck with snowy steamed buns surrounding it; and shiny jade-green vegetables with black mushrooms. There were also little barbecued birds, one for each person at the table.

"Are these baby chickens?" I asked.

"Quail," Uncle Shin said.

By now, I was no longer shocked by anything we ate. Compared with all the other foods I had eaten, quails were pretty ordinary.

"You notice how there are a lot of birds for dinner?" Uncle Flower said. "The quails, chicken, and duck? They are to symbolize the phoenix, which is the mythical bird that represents the empress. Having all these birds is a way to honor Grandma."

"Really?" I asked.

"I should know," Uncle Flower said. "I listened to your Auntie Jin talk about the menu for months and months."

In the center of the table, on a big plate that matched the design of the rice bowl gifts, there was a mountain of yellow noodles stir-fried with meat and slices of green onions.

"And you have to have this," Uncle Flower said, putting a big scoop of noodles on my plate. He had to lift his arms high in the air to make sure the long noodles didn't touch the tablecloth.

"Why?" Ki-Ki asked.

"Because they are long-life noodles," Uncle Flower said. "It's a tradition for birthdays."

"Why?" she asked again.

"They say there was a man who lived to be eight hundred years old," Uncle Flower said. "He had a very, very long face. *Mianchang* is the word for 'long noodles,'

platter of long-life noodles

and it sounds like the word for 'long face,' too. So, by eating these noodles we hope we will live as long as the long-faced man."

"He really lived to be eight hundred years old?" I said.

"Who knows?" Uncle Flower said. "But people have been eating noodles for even longer than that."

So far, Grandma's birthday party was a lot like Clifford's wedding, which we went to last year. Everything was in Chinese and Taiwanese, and there was a lot of food and a lot of people — mainly adults, too.

Then suddenly, the lights began to flicker. *BANG-ba-ba-ba-BANG! BANG!* A deafening, rhythmic banging thundered through the room and made us all jump. I covered my ears with my hands. The sound seemed to push people away, and we could see a drummer standing at the front of the room hitting a large drum as tall as his waist. *BANG-ba-ba-ba-BANG! BANG!* It was so loud! I saw the muscles in the drummer's arms with each strike.

"What's going on?" Ki-Ki said, clinging to Mom. But Mom didn't have a chance to answer, because two huge Chinese lions came springing into the room!

I had never seen the Chinese lion dance before in person. I had seen photos of it and parts of it on TV, but never right in front of me. I knew they were people in costume, but they really did look like strange, wild beasts. There were two bright yellow lions, the color of sunflowers, with patterns of sparkling sequins and wavy hair. Their giant, fur-trimmed eyes made up most of their oversize heads. Designs of shiny gold, red, and black were painted all over. Pom-poms like fuzzy cherries bounced over their noses and round horns grew out of the tops of their heads. But it was their large, grinning mouths full of painted teeth that made you feel like you couldn't trust them.

lion dance

The lions jumped and darted back and forth, sometimes in unison, sometimes at each other. You couldn't tell if they were playing or attacking or if their mouths were laughing or snarling. Every movement was to the loud *BANG-ba-ba-ba-BANG! BANG!* of the drum, until it seemed like they were just flashes of gold and red.

"I don't like it!" Ki-Ki said loudly. Her voice filled the gaps of sound in between the drumming.

"Shhh!" I hissed at her, and Lissy nudged her, too. "Stop! That's rude!"

Ki-Ki didn't care. She scrunched her eyes and covered her ears tightly. She didn't scream, but I could tell that most of the guests had seen her by the amused smiles on their faces. My face burned with embarrassment. I heard someone ask Uncle Shin a question in Chinese.

"*Meiguo*," Uncle Shin replied.

"Ah." The person nodded. "*Meiguo hua qiao.*"

American. Again. Now Ki-Ki had made us look like we were a bunch of babies and almost ruined the show. Somehow we were always doing something wrong.

But the booming drum made any kind of talking impossible, and the bright colors of the leaping and swaying lions were hypnotizing. With a final *BANG-ba-ba-ba-BANG! BANG! BANG! BANG!* the two lions fell to the floor at Grandma's feet. As the silence soaked through the room, it was replaced by loud clapping and cheering. The lions stood up, shook off their bodies, and took off their heads. Underneath, grinning, were Uncle Flower, Shogun, Julian, and their father! This was what they had been practicing all the time! This was the secret! I was a little jealous.

Everyone clapped even louder, and Grandma and Grandpa jumped to their feet to hug them. People started getting up and walking around. The waiters began to put new dishes on the table and serve tea. We followed Uncle Shin to the front of the room.

"You were really good!" I said to Julian. She was younger than me, but she was just as tall. The small hairs that had escaped her braid were moist from her sweat. She was still a little out of breath, but she gave us a shy smile and her eyes lit up so that they looked like the inside of a poppy flower.

"Thank you," she said.

"Everyone liked it!" I said. It was hard to think of what to say that she would understand. "Well, except Ki-Ki. I think she was scared."

"Ki-Ki, lion," she said. "Not used."

"Yes," I said. "She wasn't used to the Chinese lions."

"Not used," Julian said. "No like."

"Yeah, you don't like things you aren't used to," I said, and then I stopped. That wasn't really true. I hadn't been used to sushi, but now I kind of liked it. And I hadn't been used to wax apples or the subway or the markets or sugarcane juice, and those were some of my favorite things. I hadn't been used to Taiwan, but now I liked it, too.

Uncle Flower said something to Julian in Chinese, and the waiters began serving the peach buns and the turtle cakes. Julian and Shogun went to change out of their costumes, and Lissy and I went back to the table. Ki-Ki was already sitting there, completely happy now that the lions were gone. The peach buns looked prettier than I remembered them, pink and white and soft. The turtle cakes didn't look as much like a turtle as I thought they would. Since the peach buns looked so realistic, I was expecting the turtle cakes to be green with a head and a tail. But the turtle cakes were flattish ovals and shiny red and sticky-looking, as if they were made of Jell-O.

The molded turtle pattern on top of the cakes made them look like oversize plastic jewels from Ki-Ki's Barbie doll.

Mom cut one of the turtle cakes into pieces, and I saw it

turtle cakes

was filled with red-bean paste, just like the peach buns. But before I could take a bite, Uncle Shin was at the front of the room again making a speech, with Grandma and Grandpa standing behind him. He was speaking in Taiwanese, and he called Aunt Bea, Auntie Jin, Uncle Flower, Shogun, Julian, and their father to stand next to him. It was probably to praise them for doing such a good lion dance. Everyone was clapping, and I felt a little jealous again, as well as a little ashamed. All the uncles and aunts and cousins had done great things for this party, and we hadn't done anything — except for Ki-Ki to be scared of the lions. We were from *Meiguo*, and I felt like we had made America look bad.

But then I heard Uncle Shin say, "Lissy, Pacy, and Ki-Ki!"

Mom walked forward, motioning us to follow. But before we moved, Auntie Jin shoved a bag at Lissy. "Give Grandma her gifts now," she whispered. I had forgotten about my painting. There it was, rolled up in the bag with another cylinder and a small flat board. Those must be Lissy's and Ki-Ki's gifts. I wondered what they were.

We all gave both Grandpa and Grandma hugs, and then

Lissy stepped forward and took out the paper cylinder from the bag and gave it to Grandma. "Happy birthday," Lissy said. Grandma unrolled it. It was a poster of Lissy! It was from her photo shoot! She was in that blue Chinese dress, holding an oiled umbrella, and smiling flirtatiously at the audience. The real Lissy turned bright pink, but everyone clapped and Grandpa said "So beautiful!" while Grandma hugged her.

Lissy handed me the bag, and I took out my painting. Grandma didn't even unroll it before she hugged me. Her face wrinkled into a hundred smiles. Someone said something to her in Chinese, urging Grandma to show everyone my painting. When she did, a flattering cry of "ohh!" went all across the room before another round of applause. I knew the painting was good. The pink birds and the bamboo all seemed to glow together.

I gave the bag to Ki-Ki, who took out her flat board. It was covered with gold paint and sparkles. It was very shiny. Ki-Ki had written in big letters #1 GRANDMA. I laughed. Ki-Ki had made Grandma an award! She probably got the idea from winning her ribbon.

After hugging Ki-Ki, Grandma held up the award for everyone to see. She lifted it over her head, like a prize-winning boxer, and laughter thundered through the room as people clapped at the same time.

"I didn't know that we'd be giving the gifts in front of

everyone," Lissy said. "I wouldn't have given Grandma the poster if I knew that."

"Why?" I said. "Grandma liked it. The poster was a good idea."

"You think so?" Lissy said, looking relieved.

I nodded. Giving Grandma the poster meant I wouldn't have to see a huge version of a weird-looking Lissy hanging at home. To me, it was a great idea.

"*Gau! Gau!*" a guest said to Mom, nodding toward us. Mom beamed. She looked just like Ki-Ki after she had won the blue ribbon.

"What did he say?" I asked Mom. "What does *gau* mean?"

"It means 'talented,'" Mom said. "He said you all are very good."

I smiled. Inside, I felt cozy and warm as if I were a soup dumpling myself. In fact, I felt like I was going to burst with happiness, I felt so glad. We were good. Even though we were Americans and we didn't speak Chinese, people in Taiwan still liked us.

And, I realized, that was what the three birds on the bamboo had been wishing for. Lissy, Ki-Ki, and I had been wishing to like Taiwan and for Taiwan to like us. The wish had come true. Some parts of Taiwan, like Grandma and Grandpa, even loved us.

But I couldn't think anymore, because Grandpa was motioning me, Lissy, Ki-Ki, and the cousins toward him and Grandma. Now what? As we came forward, Grandma reached into her purse and gave us each a bright red envelope, the color of the last roses of summer. "*Hong bao*," Mom said. "Lucky money. It's a gift."

We got gifts on Grandma's birthday? That seemed backward, but no one else thought it was odd. Lissy, Ki-Ki, and I grinned at one another. We had never gotten birthday presents at someone else's birthday party before, but we liked it. I knew we weren't supposed to open gifts in front of people, but I couldn't help sneaking a peek inside the envelope. Grandma had given us American money, and I counted three twenty-dollar bills! That was sixty dollars! *Wow!* She must have given us sixty dollars because she was sixty years old. We each rushed up to Grandma and Grandpa to thank them.

"I hope we come to your birthday every year!" I said to Grandma.

She gave me a big hug. "Me, too," she said.

Good-bye!

suitcase
with things
from Taiwan

AND THEN IT WAS THE LAST DAY. INSTEAD OF DOING anything fun, all we did was pack. It was very hectic packing all our things. I hadn't thought we had bought that much new stuff, but not everything fit in our suitcases, and Mom ran out to get another bag. And we had filled the extra suitcase we had used to bring gifts from the U.S., too.

There *was* a lot of new stuff. Every time we put something in, I kept thinking, *It's the last day. It's the last day.* We didn't want to forget anything. Everyone's projects from class, our

tin of plum candy

name chops, our lucky money. Mom kept jamming in extra packs of seaweed and rice crackers. We all kept grabbing and packing food that we knew we couldn't get in New Hartford. Lissy bought ten tins of sour plum candy, and Ki-Ki took bags of white melon

candy. I didn't bring candy, but I did ask
Mom if we could go back to the bakery
for more pineapple cakes. She said yes,
and we rushed all the way there to get
them.

melon candy

Of course, there were lots of things we couldn't bring.
We couldn't pack our three goldfish. Those would have

goldfish looking

to stay behind, and they seemed to know
it. Whenever we passed the bowl, the
fish looked at us with big, reproachful
eyes.

And we couldn't bring back Aunt Bea
or Auntie Jin or Grandma or Grandpa, either. Somehow, going home made me feel sad. I was glad to be going back to
where everyone spoke English, where I could call Melody on
the phone, see Becky and Charlotte, and peek at Sam Mercer. And New Hartford had our comfortable white house
with the green shutters, clean wind, and trees that grew as
if they could hug the sky. But I'd also miss the stories Uncle
Flower told us, the hugs from Grandma and Grandpa, and
Auntie Jin's morning smile. I'd miss Taiwan's rich, thick air
full of food smells and the window we looked out of at night
to see the city lights brighten the sky like stars. New Hartford and the United States was still my homeland. But I had
gotten to feel at home in Taiwan.

I wondered if the ghosts felt that way, too. "Ghost Month

is ending," Auntie Jin said that night. "So soon there'll be no more burning things on the streets. The ghosts are going home."

Like us, I thought.

And then the next morning, Lissy, Ki-Ki, and I were wearing our pink over-all dresses again. They didn't fit that well. Lissy's was so short that she wore plaid shorts underneath. I felt like a too-full water balloon in mine, and Ki-Ki's had a button that kept popping open.

Lissy wearing shorts under her dress

Our suitcases closed, surprisingly, and stood behind us like a castle wall. We had to call for a special, extra-large

Grandma hugs Mom good-bye

taxi. It was really a van, not a taxi. As it arrived, Grandma and Grandpa hugged and kissed us good-bye—a small silver tear, the size of the head of a pin, silently dropped from the corner of Grandma's eye onto Mom's shoulder. Aunt Bea, Auntie Jin, Aunt Yoko, Auntie Kim, Shogun, and Julian waved as the taxi pulled away, and we kept waving, turning around in our seats to see them through the back window.

"So are you happy to be going back?" Uncle Shin asked us. He and Uncle Flower were going to the airport with us.

"Yes and no," Lissy said.

"It's forever like that," Uncle Shin said. "For me, as soon as I am in Taiwan, I miss the United States. When I am in the U.S., I miss Taiwan."

"It's because we're both," I said, thinking about my name chop. America and Taiwan. English and Chinese. "We're mixed up."

"Uh-huh," Uncle Shin said. "But I wouldn't want it any other way. Would you?"

Would I want it any other way? Would I want to live in New Hartford and not know that peaches meant long life or the taste of a soup dumpling? Or to live in Taiwan and not know about Thanksgiving turkeys or what a real McDonald's hamburger was like?

"No," I said. "I'm happy this way."

The taxi arrived at the airport, and we pushed and pulled our luggage out and through the terminal. When we got to the part of the airport where Uncle Shin and Uncle Flower couldn't follow, there were good-byes all over again. This was the last good-bye. Mom sighed before she gave Uncle Shin and Uncle Flower a hug, and I thought I saw a tear, like a dropping pearl, fall from her eye. It was just like Grandma's when we said good-bye. Ghost Month was over, but I had learned that some ghosts never leave.

plastic bag

Uncle Flower shoved a tightly tied plastic bag at me. "Here," he said. "Don't open it until you are on the plane."

"What is it?" I asked.

"A good-bye present," he said. "Your Auntie Jin told me to give it to you."

Then he smiled, and he and Uncle Shin pushed us forward. As we walked away, we waved using our whole arms, as if we were saying good-bye to all of Taiwan, not just them. We turned the corner, and they disappeared from our sight. It was time to go.

On the airplane, Mom let me have the seat closest to the window first. "Since you asked first," Mom said. "But you have to share. In the middle of the flight, you and Lissy can switch."

"We're going to be flying forever! Ugh!" Lissy grumbled. "I don't mind being home or being in Taiwan—it's getting there that I don't like."

Uncle Flower and Uncle Shin waving good-bye

The flight attendant began to give the talk on airplane safety. We all watched in silence, even though it was in Chinese. She gave it again in English, and we still said nothing. I felt that all of us, even Ki-Ki, were thinking about how our month in Taiwan was now ending.

The airplane began to move. Faster and faster, the landscape blurred. Then, as if the airplane were taking a deep breath, we were up in the air.

"Are you sad?" I asked Mom.

"No," she said. "Well, a little."

I was, too. I wished I could think of something to say. I pulled at my bright pink dress and thought about how we were pink birds again, this time flying home. What had Dad said about traveling, so long ago? "You take something with you, you leave something behind, and you are forever changed," he had said. "That is a good trip."

Our trip to Taiwan had been a good trip, then. We were taking a whole extra suitcase of things with us, and we had left our gifts to Grandma and our goldfish behind. But was I forever changed? In my painting, there were pink birds on bamboo with a chop mark that said "forever." I was one of the pink birds, and I had wished on the bamboo to like Taiwan. It had happened. My changed feelings for Taiwan would be forever.

I thought about the fortune-teller who had given me her blessing. She had said her blessing would help me and make me happy. Mom had said it was a lot of nonsense, but I was

259

glad she had blessed me. Maybe it was her blessing that helped me live with my ghosts and find my identity. Maybe it was her blessing that helped me like Taiwan and Taiwan like me. I kicked at the bags at my feet.

"What's that bag?" Mom said, pointing at the tightly wrapped plastic bag.

"I don't know," I said. "Uncle Flower gave it to me. He said it was a good-bye gift and not to open it until I was on the plane."

"Well, open it!" Lissy said.

I untied the plastic bag and took out a large Chinese food container with a pair of chopsticks taped to it. The container was still warm, and the heat spread to my lap. I took off the chopsticks and opened the flaps, and inside were . . .

DUMPLINGS!

We all laughed.

"The summer, all those days in Taiwan — it was fun, wasn't it?" Mom asked.

"Yes," I said, nodding. This time, Mom's idea of fun was exactly the same as mine. "It was."

all the different dumplings I had in Taiwan

xiaolongbao
(soup dumplings)

xia jiao
(shrimp dumplings)

shaomai
(pork dumplings)

gyoza
(Japanese dumplings)

qu han jiao er tang
(Chinese dumpling
soup)

jiaozi
(Chinese
dumplings)

mochi
(Japanese dessert
dumplings)

A Note from the Author's Parents

WHEN WE READ THIS BOOK, IT BECOMES THE SUMMER, MANY, many years ago when we, with our daughters, returned to Taiwan.

Before returning, our memories were filled with farmers on the greenish rice paddies and the blue sky. But that was a dreamland, for Taiwan had quickly matured into the rows of high-rises, busy streets, buses, and crowded subways. However, it was still our people, our culture, and our homeland.

But reading the return through our daughter's eyes brought back our surprise as well as showing us even more. There were so many things that we thought our children would know—from holding chopsticks to using the toilets—just because we did. Reading this book reminded us how strange the familiar could be. We had thought that bringing our daughters to Taiwan was simply a good experience, one for them to enjoy. We did not expect it would be one of discovery as well.

The Taiwanese people are extremely warm and close-knit. It is a small island, and people are somehow always connected. There are no boundaries, and people open their hearts, wishing to meet yours.

Dumpling Days captures this and much more. This is the most memorable book for us because reading it is like coming home. Please come and visit our home.

You are very welcome here.

Jer-Shang & Lin-Lin Yang Lin

Chinese Dumplings

by Lin-Lin Yang Lin

(makes approximately 50 dumplings)

Ingredients:

For wrappers:
1 ½ cups lukewarm water
5 cups flour

For filling:
1 pound ground pork
1 tablespoon pepper
2 teaspoons salt
1 tablespoon sugar
2 tablespoons sesame oil
3 tablespoons soy sauce
2 tablespoons garlic powder
⅓ cup chopped green onion
½ pound salt-treated, chopped, boiled Chinese greens (napa
    cabbage) with as much liquid removed from them as possible
    (Hint: Twist a clean towel around them and squeeze.)
1 beaten egg

Method:

Make the wrappers:
1. Add the water into the flour, and mix well. Knead the dough until it is smooth.
2. Place the dough in a clean bowl, and cover the bowl with a damp cloth. Let the dough sit for 30 minutes.
3. Knead the dough again, then roll a portion into a log shape. Cut the log into slices, and roll the slices into balls. Repeat with the remaining dough as necessary. You should have about 50 balls.
4. Sprinkle flour onto your rolling surface, and roll out the balls into flat, round shapes (like small pancakes), about 1/8 inch thick.
5. Sprinkle some flour onto both sides of those flat wrappers.

Make the meat filling:
1. In a big bowl, mix the ground pork, pepper, salt, sugar, sesame oil, soy sauce, garlic powder, and green onion, and stir until the mixture is well blended.
2. Add the chopped Chinese greens into the pork mixture. Mix well until blended thoroughly.

Make the dumplings:
1. Place a small spoonful of the filling mixture onto a wrapper. Lightly brush the edges of the wrapper with the egg.
2. Fold the wrapper, and seal it into your desired dumpling shape. Repeat until you've run out of either the mixture or the wrappers.
3. Line up the dumplings on a lightly floured tray.

Cook the dumplings:
1. Fill a pot with water and bring it to a boil. Place the dumplings in the water, and make sure all the dumplings are submerged. Cover the pot until the water boils again.
2. Add a cup of cold water, and let it boil again.
3. Take out the dumplings, serve them with soy sauce (as another option, add chopped garlic or sliced ginger), and eat!

Behind the Story of Dumpling Days

Dumpling Days was inspired by my first trip to Taiwan, but it really is a mix of all the trips I've taken there since my youth. A lot of the things that I wrote about did not happen on my first trip to Taiwan, but trips that happened afterward. I still go back to Taiwan now, and a lot of the things that I saw on my first trip are still there!

However, on my very first trip, my mother did make my sisters and me wear matching pink dresses:

And I really went to an English-speaking camp where I took art lessons:

And I did eat a lot of dumplings! I still eat and love dumplings today, and Taiwan serves the best (in my opinion). Now, some even come with directions on how to eat them. I wish they had that when I was younger.

The Night Market is still there, too. Every night it's still full of people, things to buy and do:

From the "frog egg" drinks:

To net-fishing game:

If you go to Taiwan, you should go see Taipei 101, like Pacy. However, in real life, I didn't visit this when I was a child (it didn't exist then). I saw it when I was older:

And many times since then! I've even brought my own daughter:

Another thing that happened when I was older was having my glamour photos done! Just like Lissy in the book:

Lissy's photo

Ha-ha! I hope you enjoyed Pacy's travels in Taiwan and maybe, someday, you will go there yourself!

Uncle Flower and Uncle Shin
waving good-bye